Unavailable

Secrets 1

Ella Sheridan

Also Available By Ella Sheridan

Secrets
Unavailable
Undisclosed
Unshakable

Southern Nights
Teach Me
Trust Me
Take Me

Southern Nights: Enigma
Come For Me
Deceive Me
Destroy Me

If Only
Only for the Weekend
Only for the Night
Only for the Moment

∞

For news on Ella's new releases, free book opportunities, and more, sign up for her monthly newsletter at ellasheridanauthor.com.

Editor: Rory Olsen
Cover Artist: Eva Talia
Published in the United States of America

Praise for *Unavailable*

"An erotic gem. It is well-written, flows at a nice pace and is chock-full of pure desire."
— *Harlequin Junkie*

"There was plenty of drama, suspense, smut factor, and of course just regular romance that will keep you turning the pages! My one complaint is that I wished the story was longer!"
— *Crystal's Many Reviews*

"This is my first book by Ella Sheridan and I can honestly say, I was blown away... Everything about this book clicked. It was perfect."
— *Nice Ladies Naughty Books*

"This story completely captured me from the very beginning and kept my attention until the very end. Cailin has a naughty side that no one but Alex ever got to experience, and once he got a taste, he did not want to give her up. I can honestly say that the relationship between those two was something out of my fantasies."
— *Long and Short Reviews*

Dedication

To Gina L. Maxwell, for telling me how you really felt about the original version of this book. You were correct, as always, girlie. I'm proud of you and all you have accomplished.

∞

And to Dani Wade, for putting up with my constant neuroses, and not just because we're family and you've had to put up with me from the time we were in the womb together. You are my rock: hard, uncomfortable—sorry, wait—solid, supportive. (Seriously, that's what I meant to write!) Always pushing me to do what needs to be done, what will make me excel, not necessarily what would make things easy. A handhold when I feel like I'm slipping. Thank you for being my sister and my best friend. Words can't express how much I love you.

Chapter One

What the heck am I doing here?

The warm summer breeze caressed Cailin's bare—very bare—thighs. Her new black sheath dress, a "knockout" according to the teenage assistant at the mall, lingered just below the crease of her...um...rear, with no intention of going any lower. Revealing cutouts along her back, rib cage, and what little there was of the skirt were lined with silky mesh material that stretched over her curves. At twenty-eight, she wasn't too old to wear young clothes, but she felt more and more naked with every passing minute.

Atlanta had an active twentysomething party scene, and it seemed as if every participating member had shown up for the grand opening of the latest downtown hot spot, Thrice. Nerves fluttered in her stomach and down her wobbly legs as she waited in the long line to enter the rocking new nightclub. Moving to Atlanta was a huge step for this small-town Alabama girl, but she'd made it. The transfer had been approved the same day her divorce finalized. At the time, Cailin hadn't been sure whether to celebrate or bawl her eyes out, but she'd done enough bawling in the year it took to divorce Sean to last more than one lifetime. The past twelve months had been hell, and all she'd wanted was a chance to start over. A clean slate.

And look where it had landed her. In line. At a *bar*.

Here she was, a long way from the provincial town she'd grown up in, alone in a city she'd only rarely visited, surrounded by strangers, and…free. Being on her own was oddly freeing. She was learning things about herself that she'd never realized before. Good things.

And then there were the things she wished would go away, like the idea she'd woken up with this morning.

Anonymity wasn't always a good thing. It tempted people to act in ways they normally wouldn't, to indulge in fantasies they'd normally never consider if someone they knew was around to see—and condemn—them. Cailin had lain awake last night, staring at the darkened ceiling, alone and hungry. And not for food. Two years was a long time to go without touch, much less sex—especially when she'd spent half that time married—and she found her craving was getting harder and harder to ignore. Taking care of it herself just didn't feel the same. She wanted human interaction, a man's hands on her body. And this morning, she'd awakened with an idea of how to get it.

Thus the trip to Crazyville, um, Thrice.

It was risky, at least for her. Definitely unhinged. She'd been a virgin on her wedding night. She didn't do casual sex. Or she hadn't, but what other choice did she have? And it just so happened she had a really long, empty weekend ahead of her and a new nightclub opening not twenty minutes from her home. Best of all, nobody knew her. Nobody would be watching her "moral slipup," as her mother would've called it. And nobody would talk. She could go, have a drink, maybe meet someone. Maybe go home with him. That's what normal people did, right? At least, people who didn't marry right out of school and who'd never in their life set foot in a bar.

What a backwoods idiot she was. She just prayed, after the amount of money she'd blown on her outfit, that the backwoods part of her was well hidden—and that this little foray into mental illness was somehow successful.

"You do realize you're asking God for a hookup, Cailin," she told herself, ignoring the questioning look of a cute young thing with a ring in his nose passing on his way to the end of the line. "That just proves how crazy you really are."

The cutie did a quick twist to stare at Cailin as he went by. His gaze zeroed in on what she knew was a mostly bare back and clearly outlined butt. Her garters played peekaboo through the cutouts, extending just below her hemline to catch sheer thigh-high stockings, but the woman at the store had assured her it was utterly sexy. Cailin didn't know about that— *naughty* might be a better word, but when had she ever been naughty? It was definitely past time to give herself a break from the good-girl routine. Tonight she could be anyone she wanted to be—and the woman she wanted to be was a sexy siren, ready to entice. Tilting a look over her shoulder, she gave the guy a smile, ignoring the jittery feeling in her stomach. Maybe she'd see him inside.

A group of women in line ahead of her giggled when the man winked back at her. They struck up a conversation about her dress, and by the time she greeted the broad-shouldered bouncer a half hour later, it felt as natural as buying a ticket to a movie. The way he eyed her legs helped her relax even more.

She couldn't swear, but she was pretty sure her reaction to that look was something like preening.

"Well, ready or not, here we go!" she whispered as she walked through the wide double doors.

The inside of the club was everything she'd ever imagined a bar to be: dark corners, flashing lights, driving music. The beat hit her middle, and the urge to dance struck hard. Since the dance floor was below the entry, almost like a sunken pit in the middle of the room, she skirted it to look around for a few minutes, fortifying herself with a fruity drink complete with miniparasol before approaching the stairs to go below.

∞

"Alex! You made it!"

In a dark corner of the club's bar, Alex Brannigan settled his frosty mug of even darker beer on the table and stood to bump knuckles with Damien, his childhood friend and owner of Thrice, before he wrapped the other man in a back-thumping bro hug. "Of course. Wouldn't miss it; you know that."

Damien flashed his signature pretty-boy smile, one Alex knew for a fact was a hundred percent genuine, gestured him back to his seat, and took the other one. "So what do you think?" He waved a hand to indicate the noisy room. "Great, isn't it?"

"You've done a phenomenal job." It was the truth. The place was a crush. Packed to the rafters, with every table full, the bar overrun, and the dance floor wall-to-wall mania. Damien's infamous Midas touch was showing again. No one would have guessed that what used to be a dilapidated old warehouse could be turned into the trendiest nightclub in Atlanta. No one but Damien. Alex's friend had an eye for the unusual, as he'd proven with his last two clubs, one in LA and the other in Denver. Hence the name.

Alex took a sip of the bitter beer, letting it soak into his taste buds as they discussed the renovations. Damien's love for his work shone through, and Alex's chest ached with envy. Not too long ago, he'd had the exact same enthusiasm for what he did, working his way to the top of the corporate ladder with the speed of an express elevator. He still loved the job itself, but at his level it wasn't just about the job. It was about the politics, and God knew he was eyeballs-deep in the shit of politics. With no way out. Not without hurting the people he cared for the most.

"So what do you think of Atlanta so far?" his friend finally asked him, rubbing a hand across the dark stubble shadowing the lower half of his face.

"It's definitely not LA."

Damien laughed. "No, it's not. But it has its moments." Two skimpily clad women sauntered by, their hips swinging in opposite directions like clashing bells. Damien watched their progress with a less than professional eye. "Yep, definitely has its moments."

Alex chuckled, shook his head, and finished off his beer with a final swallow.

Damien's unrepentant grin gave the totally false impression of an innocent little boy; only the strong edge to his jaw and the hungry look in his eyes gave away the lie. "Hey, there's a reason I do what I do." His expression turned greedy as he surveyed the female population weaving around them. "And the nice thing about the women here? They're not all silicone and collagen injections. The more natural the better, I always say."

Alex silently agreed.

A waiter with a black apron around his waist approached the table. "Mr. Adams, Brad has some questions about—"

Damien raised a hand to cut the guy off, that hundred-watt smile softening the gesture. "I'm coming; give me just a minute." He turned to Alex, clapping him on the back as he rose. "You won't be a stranger, will you? I'll have Brad send over another beer." He nodded at Alex's empty glass.

"Thanks, but I've got to head back." It had been a long day in an even longer week, but he hardly knew what else to do with his time anymore but work. He stood and walked with Damien toward the bar. "Congratulations, man. Thrice looks like a helluva success."

"Yeah, it does, doesn't it?"

Alex gave the man a rueful grin. "And that's what we've always loved about you: your humility."

Damien barked out a laugh, then headed behind the bar.

Alex started the long walk toward the front door. The bar area was situated above the dance floor, which was sunk a whole level underground, the overhang surrounded with a wrought-iron balcony of sorts that allowed partygoers to watch the action below before deciding to dive in. He stopped at the edge, leaned his forearms on the hard railing, and let himself get lost in the mindlessness of writhing bodies and pulsing rhythms for just a few minutes.

Women glanced up, over, and around, his dark good looks drawing them in. He knew what they saw; he saw it in the mirror every day. A stranger. The crisp, dark hair, brown eyes, engaging smile—they belonged to someone he didn't recognize anymore. Inside he was numb, hanging in a limbo that dulled the hungry edge with which he usually tackled life, completely disconnected from the successful business persona that conquered anything put in his path. Oh, he knew why, understood what the problem was, but he couldn't fix it. Just wallow in it, hide it, and hate himself the whole time.

He shook his head and straightened, turning toward the door. He had to get back to the office before he got downright maudlin, and that he would never accept, ever.

The wide glass doors leading out to the street still loomed half a room away when he spotted her, the sight literally stopping him in his tracks. Thick, curly blonde hair swayed to below her shoulders, and when she pushed it back to tuck behind a delicate ear, soft caramel eyes shone in the dark of the room. She looked younger than his own thirty-six years, or maybe that was just the innocence in her unlined face talking. But her body didn't say innocent; it screamed *come take me.* All lush curves and mysterious hollows encased in a black dress that should be declared illegal for the way it conformed to her shape. Damn if his cock didn't sit up and beg with that very first glimpse. And the longer he looked, the harder he got, until every single thought vanished and all he could concentrate on was making his way toward her. He needed to know her name; he wasn't sure why, and he didn't care. Knowing was all that mattered.

Think, idiot, and with something besides your hard-on. Can you afford this?

White-knuckling the wrought iron to halt his progress, he stopped, dropped his head, forcing out the picture of her lithe form making her way down to the dance floor. *Weigh the cost. Consider the risks.* But all his brain wanted was to justify his hungry gaze on her.

The past two years had been consumed with protecting his reputation, insulating himself from innuendo, rumor, the wagging tongues that followed success—his in particular. Practicality said that at some point, he had to have another woman, if for no other reason than to relieve the constant blue balls he lived with every day. His libido shouted *yes!* at the thought, but his brain brought the tongue-hanging drive for sex to a screeching halt. His arms shook at the force of his grip on the balcony, but he refused to let go. *Think.*

He closed his eyes, letting the world around him fall slowly away. Okay, so he'd think. One, he was in a new city, one not nearly as gossip hungry as LA. Two, it hadn't been long enough for his employees to get to know him, professionally and personally, or for him to worry about what they might say. Not that he'd seen anyone he knew tonight anyway. And three, if he didn't act and act soon, he was gonna fucking do something drastic, like throw himself off the nearest bridge high enough to put him out of his misery.

That's what he told himself, anyway.

The truth was, she captivated him. No name, no conversation, not even eye contact. None of it mattered. When he raised his eyes and caught sight of her in the midst of the crowd, slender arms arched above her body as she writhed to the beat of the music, logic fled, and the heavy haze of desire demanded he have her.

Guess that answered his question. He really was losing touch with reality.

Too bad. For the first time that he could remember, Alex Brannigan threw caution completely to the wind and made a decision based solely on his dick. God forgive me, he thought as he made his way down to the lower level. There was no going back now.

A PAUSE IN the cacophony was followed by the sultry sound of a sax filtering across the dance floor. Cailin stopped to catch her breath at the sound. She hadn't been completely alone as she danced; several men had approached, partnered her for a few minutes, then left, leaving her available for another dance, another partner. She'd thought she would feel awkward dancing with strangers, but she didn't. She enjoyed it. And she didn't feel like a slut, either.

As the timbre of the music worked its way into her bones, she let her body move, sway, absorb the pleasure of sense and sound. When broad, heavy palms landed on her rocking hips, she startled. She whipped her head around, only to meet the darkest, sexiest brown eyes she'd ever seen. They blazed with emotion in a face that put Brad Pitt, Tom Cruise, and every other Sexiest Man Alive to absolute shame. Her mouth opened in a soft "oh" as she stared.

God, he was beautiful.

And then he smiled. It was soft, secretive, sexy. Steaming. Her legs wobbled beneath her, but his grip kept her upright. Then his body made contact with hers—full-body contact, her back, point by point, met by the muscled heat of his chest, stomach, thighs. A gasp escaped as his pelvis brushed the base of her spine and an unmistakably rigid bulge made itself known. The next moment, she was lost in the intensity of his touch.

Her head turned to the side, Cailin tried to smile, but nerves and something else had wicked the moisture from her lips. He moved against her, his hips more agile than Patrick Swayze's in *Dirty Dancing*, and nuzzled his sharp nose against the cheek closest to him.

"Hi."

Her head reeled, her tongue tied itself in a firm knot, and she wished the solid floor beneath her would do her a favor and swallow her whole. Fast. "Hi."

And then she gave herself up to the music. Talking was impossible, but moving wasn't. And it felt delicious. She melted into the firm body supporting her, countered the sway of his hips, and fell in love with a man she'd spoken only one word to. Of course, she only loved him for his body. Nothing could compare. Nothing could ever feel as good as he felt against her. His arms circled her waist, his hands flat on the soft curve of her stomach. She wanted them on her breasts. On her mound. Between her legs. The music made love to her, one beat at a time, and he partnered it perfectly until her brain couldn't think, couldn't tell where she ended and he began. Didn't want to. All she wanted was for this moment to last forever.

Which, of course, it couldn't.

At the music's final note, the man turned her in his arms, his tight grip pulling her into his body until her front was as firm against him as her back had been. She looked up—and up. Her head tilted back farther than she'd imagined it would have to in order to meet those chocolate eyes. He had to be at least six-four, much taller than Sean—

No, she wouldn't think about Sean tonight. In the fantasy world she'd created, Sean no longer existed. He belonged to tomorrow and reality. Now was for sweet heat and the fantasy lover staring down at her.

"I'm Alex," he said. His voice was a mix of gravel and velvet, the sound clenching her womb. Cailin blushed as a rush of hot moisture coated her inner thighs.

"Cailin."

Alex tucked his head down to hear her, and at her name, he turned, eye to eye, his wide pupils mesmerizing her. Time stopped. Sound receded. And then he wet his bottom lip with a slick pink tongue. "Nice to meet you, Cailin."

That seductive smile flashed again, so close she could touch it, taste it, before he straightened. The press of the heavy wall of his chest into her sensitive breasts brought a moan to her lips, one she abruptly cut off as soon as she realized what she'd done. *Jeez, Cailin. Get it together.* But he didn't seem to mind. In fact his eyes heated further, and he rubbed lightly against her. In the back of her mind was the thought that if anyone else had pulled that move, she would have to remove his balls with her knee, but with Alex, it felt right. She didn't know why. It just did.

Music swelled again, and Alex took control, moving her against him, the subtle rubbing of their bodies the most sensual foreplay she'd ever experienced. She knew in that moment that she would have sex with this man. If he wanted her—and the erection still going strong between them said he did—she would have him. She wouldn't lose this opportunity. Guess she'd found her courage…in his arms.

The minutes passed with no regard to how much she wanted them to pause. As the next song came to an end, she realized they were close to the edge of the dance floor. Alex stepped aside, took her hand in his, and led her toward what looked like a dark hallway heading off to one side. Cailin balked, some unwanted feminine instinct waking her to reality and danger, but Alex soothed her. "Offices. The owner's a friend of mine. I thought we could talk someplace quieter."

Turning for a last look at the crowded dance floor, she followed him down the long hall, berating herself for the stupidity of the move but unable—or unwilling—to say no. Something deep down in her soul, some gut feeling she thought she'd lost when her marriage fell to pieces, trusted this man. Maybe it was the way he seemed to read her mind, to know what she needed before she did. The way he anticipated every move, as if even a breath didn't escape his notice. She'd never felt like the center of a man's entire concentration. She wanted more, wanted to bask in the intensity of Alex's attention.

And the occasional employee passing them assured her they weren't completely alone. If she screamed, someone would hear. Wouldn't they?

A wide, heavy door marked, appropriately enough, OFFICE waited at the end of the passageway. Alex knocked, and a dark-haired man with classic playboy looks opened the door. The surprise on his face eased more of her worry. So this wasn't a regular occurrence; thank God, even if she did want to sink through the floor in embarrassment.

"Damien, could I—"

"No problem." The man didn't ask for an explanation, and his cheeky grin said he didn't need any. "Just lock up when you leave." He nodded politely at Cailin before turning to walk back the way they'd come.

Alex gave a rueful snort and dragged her inside. The minute the door clicked shut, he had her backed against its unforgiving surface.

"I'm sorry," he whispered roughly. "I need—"

Cailin kissed him before he could finish.

Chapter Two

Her mouth was sweet, silken heat. It seared his senses, fired a passion he swore he'd never felt before. He opened his mouth over hers, driving his tongue between her full lips, and entered paradise.

The door at her back was unforgiving, allowing him to feel every soft inch of her body as he pressed her into it. Firm, ripe breasts, nipples spiking into his chest. Womanly hips and belly, just the way he liked them. The hollow of her thighs nestled his sweetly, allowing him slight access to the center of her body. The only thing he couldn't feel, he grabbed with both hands—a high, full ass that yielded to his touch just enough for a firm, perfect grip. She felt faultless, fitting him like a missing puzzle piece, and her kiss tasted of heat and hunger and a desperate need to match his own.

"Cailin…"

The sound of her name faded along with his thoughts at the tentative touch of delicate fingers against his jaw. They explored the evening stubble covering his cheeks and chin, rubbed against the sharp prickles of hair marching down his throat, then drove upward to sink into the sides of his hair and grip tight as he nibbled the tip of her tongue. Panting breaths filled the space between them as they devoured each other, need mounting with every exhale. The need for more. A need he couldn't deny.

Hands shaking with the sheer force of his desire, he eased along the curve of her ass, his heart kicking at the lack of panty lines, then smoothed around to her nipped-in waist and up the soft contours of her rib cage. Losing the press of her body against his chest just about killed him, but her breasts waited, beckoning, and he needed his hands on them. Dark eyes met caramel as he palmed her, hands full and then some, and ran rough thumbs across both tight nipples. Cailin tipped her head back against the door and moaned, arching into his touch.

He was minutes, maybe seconds from the point of no return, but the memory of the innocence that rested behind her closed eyelids, such a sharp contrast to her made-for-pleasure body, had him asking, "Cailin?"

Heavy lids drifted up at his voice. She stared at the ceiling as if in a daze.

"Cailin, look at me."

Her gaze met his as her pelvis tilted forward. She ground lightly against his hard-on. "You feel so good. It's—" She clamped the rest of her sentence off behind tight lips.

He leaned his forehead against hers. "You feel good too. Too good. I need to know you're with me, Cailin. I can't…" Her mound circled against him again, and it was his turn to moan, his words trailing into the ether.

Then her lips were against his, her breath moist as she whispered into his mouth, "Yes."

He hooked his fingers in the low neckline of her dress and pulled, taking the lace of her bra with them. He could feel the rapid pounding of her heart but kept his gaze locked with hers. Passion flickered there like an old-fashioned flip book, flashes of something else playing hide-and-seek as the fabric moved lower and lower still—fear, maybe, or…no.

Embarrassment. Of her body, or of what they were doing? She wanted the sex as much as he did; he knew that. But this wasn't normal for her. The truth of that was clear in her eyes.

In seconds her breasts were on display for him, and he dropped desperate eyes to see her. Beautiful, creamy mounds with hard pink nipples stretched toward him. He traced the blue veins mapping the route to those delectable tips, circling each sensitive nub before moving along another line, then back again. Gasps of pleasure escaped Cailin's lips, rising into a wail when he gripped both nipples between fingers and thumbs and squeezed. He pulled out, milking her, lost in the dazed hunger consuming her face.

"Please!" She grabbed his head and pulled him to her. He surrounded a jutting tip with eager lips and suckled hard. Cailin screamed his name.

The last harness on his control broke in that moment. There was no going slow, no patience, no thought left. Only fast. Hard. Now. That was all he knew. Her breast in his mouth, he sent one hand seeking under the hem of her stretchy skirt. When he encountered skin, he popped off her nipple to curse soundly before taking the swollen peak lightly between his teeth and searching out the apex of her thighs.

Moist heat coated the lace at her crotch as he moved it aside. Cailin lifted a knee to ride his hip, giving him better access, and he immediately drove two fingers straight in. She bucked against him, her channel spasming around his fingers, locking him inside as her pleasure detonated like an out-of-control rocket.

The feel of her orgasm sparked emotion deep in his chest that Alex knew better than to acknowledge. Instead he rubbed her clit lightly with his thumb, setting her off again. She was tight, tighter than he'd expected, and he had to work to thrust his fingers far enough inside to stroke the rough surface of her G-spot. Cailin gasped, almost choking, her shock apparent. He swallowed the sound with a desperate kiss, wringing every nuance of pleasure from her body before releasing her mouth.

As she trembled against him, lost in the afterglow, Alex jerked desperately at the zipper of his pants, smearing her cream over the material in the process. In record time, his cock was free and hastily sheathed in a condom. He adjusted her leg higher on his thigh, bent his knees, and thrust home.

"Alex!" Her death grip on his shoulders, the nails digging deep, shouted pain, not pleasure. *Shit, shit, shit.* Not what he wanted. He stilled immediately.

"Shh. It's all right, Cailin. All right." He soothed her with murmured words and gentle kisses and soft caresses along her hips and sides, the jagged sob of her breath knotting his stomach even as he shook with the need to reach his own climax. But not at her expense.

Instead he rocked them from side to side, easing the constriction surrounding him. The wet heat of her earlier release teased his sheathed cock as he nibbled and sucked the muscle along the side of her neck. Gradually her grip changed to needy clutching as he slid his mouth down to her breast, licking one softening nipple until it stood sharp and proud once more before taking it between his lips and torturing her with pleasure. Not until her body vibrated with hunger did he begin to thrust, and the feel of her so tight around him, arching into him, grinding her clit against his pelvic bone, sent him over the edge in thirty seconds flat. Not near soon enough. Or long enough.

"Come for me, Cailin," he wheezed through the sharp contractions, sliding a hand between them and pressing hard against that sensitive nub, circling as he forced himself as deep as he could go.

"No, I can't." She rolled her head back and forth against the door, her gaze desperate, aching, lost.

"Yes, you can. Come for me." He angled his hips, the broad head of his still-hard shaft dragging along her G-spot, and with one more press on her clit, she exploded, this time around his ultrasensitive cock, amazing him when she pulled him with her once more into the abyss.

∞

"Don't."

Cailin forced herself to stillness, shoving the quiet panic that had erupted the moment he slid out of her far into the background, desperate to appear calm and worldly and sophisticated—the woman in the sexy black dress, not the woman from nowhere Alabama with zero idea how that other persona would act. It took a moment to realize she had turned away from Alex and was fumbling with the doorknob as ineffectually as he was fumbling with his clothes. Both of their hands were shaking, but Alex had stepped close to her back anyway, his heat as effective a barrier to her leaving as his words and her unsteadiness.

Alex tossed something across the room—the condom, she realized as it thunked into the trash can—his zipper slid up, and then he was holding her against him. The physical reassurance answered some unknown need deep in her chest. A hard, hiccupy sigh escaped, and her body ignored her panic and went lax against him.

The tip of his nose met the join of her jaw and neck, and he inhaled. He'd done that before, taking her in even as he took her with his body. As if he wanted to wallow in her scent. The thought brought a surge of longing—for him to desire her that way, for her to do the same to him. But that wasn't what a one-night stand was about, was it?

"I need to go," she whispered, not knowing what else to say.

He gave an adamant jerk of his head. "No." The tip of his tongue traced her pounding pulse, then, "Stay with me."

"Here? But your friend—"

He lifted his head, and she could sense awareness of their surroundings filtering in as he tensed.

"No, not here."

"Where?"

He turned her to face him, his grip firm on her waist. "Anywhere. Just for tonight." One hand rose to sweep her hair back from her face, and she caught the faint scent of her arousal as his fingertips brushed her skin. He tipped her chin up so she met his gaze. "There's just something… I don't know. I need to feel alive. I haven't felt alive in a long time." Light glinted off his eyes, and for a moment she swore tears pooled there before he blinked and the light was gone.

"Come here," he said, tugging her away from the door and toward the desk. The box of tissues sitting on the corner yielded two fluffy squares. Alex pulled her close, looked into the furthest depths of her eyes, and watched her jump as he brought the soft tissues to her wet thighs and eased the moisture away. His gaze seared her almost as much as his touch. So tender. Kind. Gentle. Everything she'd assumed a man she'd just met and jumped into sex with would not be.

She could lose forever in his eyes.

He tossed the tissues in the same direction the condom had flown.

Silence settled between them as Alex struggled for words. Finally only one escaped. "Please." There was a desperation in his voice, in his hands as they gripped her, that she didn't understand. As if he really did need her, really did want her. It was that desperation she couldn't say no to.

She let him take her hand and lead her back down the hallway, past the dance floor, and out the front doors. He signaled a passing cab, and within minutes they were at the nearest hotel.

Well, it's not a Motel 6, at least. It was easily five-star, but she couldn't help being disappointed. She'd hoped for more than the typical hotel treatment of a one-night stand, and how stupid was that? A one-night stand was exactly what this was.

She reminded herself to breathe and not fiddle as they stepped onto the elevator together. His grip on her hand anchored her until they reached their room on the sixth floor, a room dominated by a king-size bed covered in more fluffy white pillows than she'd ever seen. Immediately the thought of how to use those pillows thrust itself into her mind, and she turned away, blushing again.

Only to face a knowing smirk on Alex's handsome face.

It was the first time she'd gotten to study him in the light, and though she'd known he was big, like this he was overpowering. Tall, broad shouldered, with at least two hundred pounds of muscle being slowly revealed as he stripped his clothes off piece by piece. The lines of his body made her mouth water— not an inch of fat, just sheer masculine perfection.

Wow.

"Shower with me," he demanded as he undid the button of his trousers, then slowly lowered the zipper. Thirty seconds more and he was completely naked. And aroused. Cailin thought she'd have a heart attack—and die a happy woman.

"I…uh…"

"Come."

Every time he said that word, she wanted to, desperately.

Alex pulled her into the bathroom. The tiles chilled her bare feet as she lingered by the door, watching him start the shower. Only when steam began to form did he turn back to her. She crossed her arms over her stomach, shivering, and watched him prowl toward her.

"Clothes. Off."

"Alex—"

He laid a single rough finger against her lips. "Never mind. Let me." And he started to undress her.

Inch by inch, limb by limb, Alex revealed her soul even as he revealed her body. By the time she stood in her garter and stockings, he'd stripped her of every bit of armor she had. Nothing could protect her from the assault on her senses. And when his fingers slipped beneath the thin straps resting against her thighs and traced the naked skin beneath, she didn't want it to. All she wanted was more.

"So pretty." Alex took her hands and drew them out to her sides, stepping back to peruse her nakedness. A brief rush of sadness filled her. She would never be stick thin, her body's natural inclination favoring curves, but her belly was soft and flat. Four years without birth control. She should have been a mother; Sean had wanted her to be a mother, blamed her for not succeeding. It was one of the reasons she'd divorced him. The constant blame had taken its toll on her heart.

But the appreciation in Alex's gaze eased that remembered pain, just a little bit. Her body pleased him, just like it was, not for what it could give him. It was more than she had gotten from Sean after their first year of marriage.

"Now what was that thought?" Alex asked.

"Hmm?"

He ran a finger along her brow. "That thought. What made you unhappy?"

"Oh." Cailin ducked her head. "It doesn't matter anymore."

Alex didn't look satisfied with her answer, but he didn't push either. Instead he pulled her behind him—giving her a mouthwatering view of his tight buns—into the steamy shower stall.

If kissing in the shower were an Olympic sport, Alex would get a gold medal. The rush of hot water over their bodies matched the rush of adrenaline as his tongue met hers, tangling, melding, saturating her with his taste, his scent. Her hands came up of their own volition to trace the silky line of hair from his belly button to his pecs, where it spread into a sparse diamond from nipple to nipple. When Alex released her mouth, she lowered her chin and nuzzled his chest. God, she loved chest hair.

Alex's jaw nudged the top of her head. "Who was he?"

"Who?"

"The man who put that look in your eye."

She sighed into his skin. "You don't give up easily, do you?"

Alex's chuckle rumbled under her ear. "No."

"He was my husband."

A heavy pause met her words. Then, "Was?"

She nodded.

"Well, that explains a lot."

Jerking back, she blinked against the water in her eyes, not all of it from the shower. "What's that supposed to mean?"

Alex cupped her cheek and leaned over to whisper near the corner of her mouth. "You were very tight, Cailin." At her shiver, he shook his head. "What did you think I meant?"

She wasn't sure. And when his hand slid along her throat and down to trace her nipple, a shake of her head was the only response she could manage.

"It's been a while, hasn't it?"

Somehow the fact that he was staring at her breasts instead of her face made it easier to answer. Go figure. "Yeah."

"Good. Because I don't even want to think about another man touching you." His free hand joined the play at her breasts. "I don't want you thinking about

28

it. I want you focused on me and only me. As if no other man ever existed." And then her mind shut down completely as he stopped talking and focused all his attention on action.

Yet no matter how much Alex whispered, touched, kissed, and plain drove her crazy, he never entered her. By the time their shower was done and he was rubbing her dry, she was quivering in the aftermath of climax, her body clenching emptily without him inside her.

The rough nap of the towel scraped across her tender, swollen nipples. "Alex," she whined.

Alex chuckled, and Cailin landed a weak smack on his wet shoulder.

"It's not funny." Her words were slurred.

Alex grabbed her hand and brought it to his lips. "I know," he murmured against it, then forced her hand down to his erect cock. "Does this feel funny?"

Cailin didn't even bother to answer; she wrapped her fingers as far around him as she could manage, the tips almost touching, and dragged upward, her clasp strong and tight. The gasp that erupted from Alex's lips was some consolation, but a heavy pulse low in her pelvis demanded more. She began to back up, pulling him along with her.

An outright laugh erupted from Alex as he willingly followed her. "Is this what they mean when they say men are led around by their dicks?"

Cailin glanced up from beneath her lowered lashes and allowed a tiny smirk to curve her lips. "Don't like it?" She squeezed just below the plum-colored crown.

Alex missed a step, then rushed her. "Definitely," he croaked out as his forward momentum tumbled them both to the waiting bed.

Lips, fingers, tongue, and teeth made steady progress down her body. When he reached her navel, Alex took his time, nipping, licking, seeming to savor her as his hands separated her thighs. Cailin relaxed, allowing her legs to spread as far as they could, the strain along her inner thighs somehow erotic, exciting. Then he leaned back to look.

Pulses of silken arousal slid from her body, down the seam of her rear, making her squirm in combined need and embarrassment. Sean had never looked at her this way. Her body had been a source of sinful pleasure, to be taken under covers in a darkened room. He'd rarely if ever touched her there, much less stared his fill with the kind of avaricious gleam so clearly evident on Alex's hungry face. When his tongue stretched out to catch the evidence of her desire, drawing it into his mouth, and his eyes closed as he savored her taste, Cailin jerked with tiny explosions of pleasure that detonated around her clit.

Alex leaned forward, clearly ready for more, but she stopped him with a hand to his stubbly cheek. "I think it's your turn."

Lids lowered over his wicked eyes, a hooded look that tingled its way up to her tight, needy breasts. Cailin didn't give him time to deny her. She turned, scooting to the side, and patted the space where she'd been. Two could play at this game. "Please."

Alex grabbed several pillows from the head of the bed and mounded them behind him, reclining just enough for comfort but still keeping a keen eye on her as she knelt on the floor between his knees. She couldn't help but stare at the thick column rising before her. Darkened skin covered his engorged shaft, giving it an angry appearance belied by the clear stream of liquid meandering from the slit at the top. Her mouth watered, and without awaiting his consent, she leaned into his body and set her tongue to his shaft, licking up the evidence of his need for her. Tart, slightly bitter, his precum melted across her tongue. Cailin moaned. His penis bobbed, tilting down toward her lips as if begging, and she had to comply. Only when the spongy, soft head hit the back of her mouth, filling her to the brim, did she stop to breathe.

The view up his body was gorgeous. Alex's head was thrown back, the masculine column of his neck centered by his bobbing Adam's apple, stubble marching along the strong line down to his heaving chest and rippling stomach. A dark nest of crisp hair surrounded his navel, trailed along his lower abs, and surrounded his erection as if it needed something extra to draw her attention to it. It didn't. The solid length jerked in her mouth, and Cailin swallowed, the sound that erupted from Alex's mouth causing both her throat and channel to squeeze at once.

He lifted his hips slightly, and Cailin slid down, taking more of him, trying to relax as the knob fitted itself to the opening of her throat and pushed lightly inside. Back. Forward. Then back again. Together they set up a rhythm that drove them both wild. And when Cailin reached with tentative fingers to surround the tight sac hanging below his shaft, rubbing lightly at the furred skin, Alex's muscles seized against her, and spurts of bitter cum sprayed into her throat.

"Oh shit! Cailin!"

The sight of Alex, bowed up before her, straining through his completion, seared her heart. Tears gathered, but not from the aching in her throat. From the aching in her chest. When Alex reached for her, dragging her roughly against him, she blinked the moisture away quickly.

His tongue speared inside her salty mouth at the exact moment his semihard shaft forced its way between her legs. At the touch of wet skin to wet skin, he flinched. "Just a minute," he whispered roughly and broke away, only to reappear with condom in hand. He was sheathed and inside her seconds later. Cailin lost count of the minutes as he took her, made love to her, brought her to a screaming orgasm she'd never even allowed herself to imagine existed. By the time she drifted off to sleep in his arms, she knew for certain: Alex was someone she could fall in love with. He was hers.

Chapter Three

The phone on the bedside table rang, startling Cailin out of a deep sleep. It took a moment for her drugged brain to come online, but she finally fumbled for the handset. "Hello?"

"Miss, this is your four o'clock wake-up call, per your request. Late checkout is in half an hour."

Late checkout? Turning her head, she listened with half an ear to the dial tone while she surveyed the hotel room. Pillows lay scattered with wild abandon across the thick beige carpet, bringing quickly to mind all the things she and Alex had done with those pillows through the night and early morning hours. Her aching pelvis echoed the sentiment, but the man responsible was nowhere to be found.

"Alex?"

Easing up, she replaced the receiver and moved carefully toward the bathroom, but the door stood open, lights off. Empty. She flicked the lights on and pulled open the shower door, as if he'd be standing in there in the dark with the water off.

No Alex.

It took about three more minutes to search the room with ridiculous thoroughness and realize Alex was no longer there. He'd left, and not a molecule of his presence remained. Not a business card, a note, not even a stray piece of lint from a sock. He was just…gone.

Gone. What else had she expected?

Not wanting to answer that question, even to herself, she scrambled to dress and make herself halfway presentable for the walk of shame out of the hotel. She called a cab and, ten minutes later, hurried through the lobby with her head firmly down to meet it, promising herself the whole time she would not cry.

She kept that promise until she stepped into the shower at home.

The heat of the water mingled with her tears until Cailin's face was so swollen she couldn't breathe. She scrubbed every inch of her sore body, taking inventory of each bruise, strawberry, burn mark from the stubble along Alex's jaw. Yeah, that appeared in some embarrassing places, places she was forced to pat dry carefully after using all the hot water and stepping, shivering, into the cool air-conditioning to run a towel over her body. Avoiding the mirror was difficult but necessary. She'd seen enough of the evidence, and if she didn't have to look herself in the eye for about ten years or so until she got over her stupidity, she'd be perfectly happy with that.

What an idiot she'd been. And was.

Numb, acting on autopilot, she made herself dinner and sat in front of the TV, her plate untouched before her. The screen could have been channeling messages from God—primarily about her coming judgment, more than likely—and Cailin wouldn't have flinched. She'd switched off at some point. And would probably be thankful for that if she could feel anything at all. But she couldn't.

Tomorrow was her first day at her new position with Keane Industries. Knowing that made it easy to abandon food and TV and thinking and climb under the covers instead, carefully setting her alarm clock, then burying her head in the blankets and allowing the world to drift away. Her last thought was to wonder where Alex was sleeping—and with whom.

∞

The Atlanta headquarters for Keane Industries were located on the eighth floor of a multistory building situated in the thriving financial center of downtown Atlanta. Cailin held her breath as she walked off the elevator to a complete wall of glass panels displaying a breathtaking—and for someone with a severe phobia of heights, bloodcurdling—vista of the surrounding city. She turned as quickly as possible and made her way toward the receptionist's desk across the entryway.

"Cailin Gray," she told the young redhead behind the desk.

"Hey, Cailin, so happy to see you, hon. We've been expecting you. Transferring to the big city, huh?" the receptionist asked with a sweet smile. Her Southern drawl was the strongest Cailin had ever heard, which was saying something considering she'd lived in the South all her life, but she withheld her wince and smiled instead as the woman tucked a loose strand of fiery hair behind one ear and consulted a computer screen to her left. "I believe Mr. Brannigan has an off-site meeting first thing this morning, which will give you a bit of settling-in time. I was fixin' to get some coffee from the break room, so let me show you around."

An hour later the receptionist, whose name was Tammy, dropped Cailin off at the senior VP's office.

"Call me if you need anything, hear?" she said, her voice trailing behind her as she hurried down the hall. Cailin waved and stepped inside.

More of those blasted windows. Shuddering, Cailin turned her back on the floor-to-ceiling display and walked over to the desk she figured belonged to her. The surface was dark, gleaming wood, the chair behind it a cushioned showpiece that would have done Captain Kirk proud. Even the drawers opened with barely a whisper as she explored, putting her purse away and familiarizing herself with the supplies available.

She had parked herself in the plush chair and reached to turn on the computer when a noise from the inner office drew her attention. The sound, a long, low moan, whispered around the door Cailin only now noticed was slightly ajar. Concerned her new boss might be ill, she hastily stood and hurried toward his office, the thick carpet cushioning her heels as she ran.

"Sara Beth, please…"

That voice. What was it about that voice that was so familiar? She didn't know anyone in Atlanta, not really. No one except…

The door slid open with barely a sound, freezing just in time to prevent it from thudding into the ultramodern black suede wall. Cailin froze as well, outlined in the open door frame as she watched the man inside bend down and place a soft, loving kiss against the corner of the lips of the woman he held in his arms. No, she didn't know anyone in Atlanta, except this man. The man she'd given her body to, the man she'd trusted, the man who'd disappeared like a shadow in the sun while she slept in the bed they'd had sex in.

The man who now held and kissed someone else.

"Alex?" she whispered.

He shouldn't have been able to hear her, not all the way across the room. Maybe he didn't; maybe he simply heard a sound and reacted. Either way, he turned his head, hands—those rough, tender, drive-her-to-the-brink hands—still cupping the woman's delicate jaw, and fastened his gaze on her. His eyes widened with recognition. Confusion. Panic. He jerked his lying ass off the edge of the sleek chrome-and-glass desk it rested on, bumping into *her*, startling, and jerking back from them both, hands fisted as they dropped to his sides. His hissed "oh shit!" echoed in the sudden silence.

SHIT WAS RIGHT; he was neck-deep in it. Cailin stood in the door to his office, and his wife stood in his arms.

How the hell did she find me?

Sara Beth waited quietly, looking from one to the other of them as if an explanation might eventually become clear, but no sound passed her lips. It was so like her. She assessed situations, drew her own conclusions, but waited to gather all the information before deciding how to proceed. Just one of the few things that made her a successful vice president in a world that favored men. One of the things he loved about her.

And he did love her. His eyes slid closed as the enormity of the situation hit him, the reality that to Cailin, he was an adulterer, the worst of the worst, a bastard. And maybe he was—a bastard, not an

37

adulterer. Rare as it was nowadays, he and Sara Beth had what used to be termed a marriage of convenience, though less than a handful of people knew. The two of them were best friends, not lovers, and never would be. But they did have to keep up appearances, at least for now, and he'd let his dick help him forget that Saturday night. Now that decision was coming back to bite him on the ass. The worst part of it was, he couldn't explain the situation to Cailin, not without risking Sara Beth's future.

And standing here like the stupid dick he was wouldn't solve anything either. Plastering a smile on his face, he moved toward Sara Beth, clasped hands with her, and took the first steps toward the door. Damn, he should have remembered to shut it.

"Cailin, what are you doing here?"

Cailin stammered. The visible effort it was taking to get herself together gripped his heart in a vise. "Today's my first day."

Sheer, ball-gripping panic had scattered his normally sharp thoughts. It was Sara Beth who made the connection.

"You're Alex's new executive assistant! What a pleasure to meet you." She dropped his hand and advanced on Cailin, her feminine skirt swirling around her. "I'm Sara Beth Brannigan, Alex's wife."

Cailin's face paled, going sheet white and strained in seconds, and he wondered if she would actually faint—and what the hell he would do about it—but he had to give her credit for class and discretion. She squared her shoulders and greeted Sara Beth politely, exchanging pleasantries as she studiously avoided looking toward him. Were her hands shaking the way they had the first time he'd touched her? He pushed the thought away quickly, ignoring Sara Beth's questioning look.

What the hell was he going to do? The entire situation hung in a delicate balance he wasn't sure he could deal with right now, wasn't sure he wanted to deal with. He'd deliberately left Cailin without a way to contact him—he had no room in his life for a lover, even if she'd been the type to accept the only kind of arrangement he might be free to offer. She wasn't, and he couldn't. It was too dangerous, too unethical, too something he would never have considered.

Until he'd met Cailin. Until he'd touched her.

The women were moving slowly into the outer office, friendly chatter filling in his blaring silence. Sara Beth he didn't worry about; she'd happily wait until tonight to have her curiosity satisfied. But Cailin? How the hell did he handle the fact that she would work for him day in and day out, in close quarters, usually alone—he groaned silently at the thought—and not explain why this wasn't the disaster she thought it was, why he wasn't the bastard she would, rightly, to her at least, label him? How—

The outer door opened, and James Allen walked in. Good ol' boy that he was, the barrel-chested investor ignored the two women right in front of him and walked straight to Alex. "Brannigan, sorry about the change this morning. Car wouldn't start, damn thing. You know how that is."

Likely not, considering the fact that Allen's car was a stretch limo complete with driver. His assistant had called earlier to explain the wait for the company to send out a new car, asking to change the location of their meeting from Allen's office to his. "No problem, James. This works just as well for me."

After shaking the man's hand, Alex escorted him into the inner office. Pausing at the door, he hesitated for a long moment before he turned back to Cailin. Tight white lines traced the edges of her mouth, but it was the determination in her shoulders that concerned him. Determination to what? Run? Cuss him black-and-blue? Whatever it was, he had a feeling he was dangling on a very short rope; he'd have to figure out how to extend it before he ended up dropping off the cliff—or hanging himself with what was left.

He spoke carefully. "Bring us some coffee, please, Cailin. And hold my calls until lunch. We'll talk then."

Her lips pressed into a firm slash, but she didn't contradict him. "Certainly, Mr. Brannigan," she said in the perfect executive assistant's voice. "I'll be in directly."

Sara Beth walked casually toward him, snuggled against his chest, the minx, and whispered in his ear, "And we'll talk tonight."

When he looked down, a devilish light sparkled in her eyes. She tiptoed up and brushed his cheek with a light kiss. "Have a good day, love."

Love. Her nickname for him, their own private little joke. But today all he could think about was how Cailin would take it. Forcing a smile, he nodded before turning his body and his thoughts to the man waiting in his office. Anything to avoid the disaster facing him when this meeting was over.

∞

She tried to cut herself some slack; she really did. She hadn't known he was married when she slept with him. She hadn't asked... Oh God, she hadn't asked! She'd just assumed everyone would be as honest as she was, that the act of sex would make it as impossible for him to fake emotions as it did for her. She knew how hard it was to fake affection; she'd done it for the last two years of her marriage, or year if you counted only the time she'd actually had any hope of getting laid. Maybe she was just too stupid to figure out how a true expert did it.

Alex, on the other hand, had obviously mastered the art of lying with his body. She would have bet her life that the intensity of his attraction had moved beyond the physical. That he enjoyed her body had been evidenced by the fact that he could get it up; it took something more to actually interact with interest and emotion and seeming honesty. Heck, he'd missed his calling. An Academy Award-winning performance, no doubt about it.

She splashed more cold water on her face, knowing her makeup could be repaired but the red, puffy eyes would give her away immediately. And the worst part of it all? She wanted to hate him. She needed to hate him, but a small kernel of feeling hidden deep down inside just wouldn't go away. Was this how women ended up in affairs? She'd never understood it...until now. She had betrayed herself as much as she had Alex's wife—her instincts, her emotions, her desires, even her integrity were all called into question now. She felt stripped bare, exposed, waiting only for the fall of the whip to flay her soul in punishment for her sins—not by some

41

judgmental outsider, but by the honor she'd thought she possessed.

"I didn't know," she whispered, the agony almost more than she could bear.

The door to the bathroom opened. Cailin kept her head down, splashing more water, until the other woman entered the nearest stall. Then she hastily dried her face and hands and repaired her makeup as best she could. Before the woman reappeared, she was walking down the hall toward her office.

Lord help her; what the heck should she do now?

James Allen opened the door to Alex's inner sanctum as she reentered the outer office. "You too, Brannigan," he called over his shoulder. "See you next week." Turning, he closed the door and headed toward her. A quick survey of her body and a slightly lascivious grin were all the acknowledgment Cailin received as the man passed. Not surprising; there were some men for whom women were nothing more than placeholders in the business world. They only truly existed at home, barefoot and pregnant, and the woman who dared step outside that arena could be explained away if the man ignored her or simply viewed her as a sex object. A decidedly old-fashioned belief but one Cailin had encountered much too often in the South. She simply nodded at the man and held the outer door for his departure.

It didn't take long for Alex to descend. The sound of his door opening three minutes later pushed steel into her cooked-noodle spine.

"Cailin." Alex turned back into his office, leaving the door ajar, a clear command to follow. Setting down the file she'd instinctively picked up—and giving herself time to take a deep breath—she slowly crossed the office and went inside.

The wall-to-wall windows dominating the back of the room caught her in their spell immediately. *Thank God for vertigo.* She'd never been thankful for her fear of heights until today. In this moment it became the perfect excuse to stop near the door, swallow hard, and struggle to get her bearings. Oh, and avoid looking at the man seated comfortably behind the monstrosity of a desk just in front of those windows. She'd never liked modern decor anyway.

Alex's voice snapped her out of her thoughts.

"Shut the door."

She jerked her gaze to him. Alex hadn't looked up from his notes, and the dark fall of his hair obscured his eyes. Turning, she did as he asked before facing him once more.

"Come in, Cailin."

The tone was firm. Commanding. The sound triggered the memory of him demanding her to climax Saturday night, turning her inside out. She couldn't afford to think about that now. Emotion would drown her if she let it; she wouldn't give him the satisfaction.

When she moved across the room to position herself behind one of the two deep chairs standing sentry before his desk, Alex finally glanced up, dark eyes inscrutable. "Sit." Impatience was creeping into his tone. "It's not like I'm going to eat you."

For one horrified moment, Cailin thought she might burst into hysterical laughter. The pain radiating from her palms as she dug her nails in as deep as they would go staved off the reaction—

barely. The chair underneath her was a welcome support.

She hadn't realized she was looking down at her abused hands until Alex's sigh drew her attention back to him. "We need to talk."

Mentally girding her loins, she peeked up from under her lashes and asked, "About?"

"Us."

"There is no us."

She could bring herself to talk, but not to look him in the eye. It didn't matter. His gaze bored a hole into the top of her lowered head anyway. "Semantics," he growled. "You know what I mean. And would you look at me, for God's sake?"

She raised her head and stared over his shoulder, trying to blur out both his captivating features and the windows behind him. Was this her punishment? She'd walked out on her marriage, and now she was destroying someone else's. Sara Beth had seemed sweet, nice—fragile. What would happen if she found out her husband had slept with his executive assistant? Or was Cailin even the first? Maybe she was just one in a long line of women he'd fucked around with. Would that make it better or worse?

"Cailin, I don't know what to say."

Bet that didn't happen often, not to Alex. She couldn't hold back an incredulous laugh.

"It's not funny."

The reins of her control were slipping under the onslaught of emotion. "No, it's fucking hilarious, Alex. Really." And now he had her cursing. The *f* word, no less. Another first. She'd had a lot of those with him.

Pain shot through her chest, taking what little breath she could muster with it.

He held up an imperious hand. "Don't. It won't change anything. I can't—"

Can't what? Surely he didn't think… "I wouldn't even if you could. I'm not that kind of woman, Alex."

"Not that kind of woman?" Something that looked strangely like pain flashed across his face and then disappeared, buried beneath a rage that had her flinching away from him. His words struck like a lash against her skin. "Exactly what kind of woman are you then, Cailin? You fucked a man you knew absolutely nothing about. You didn't even know my last name until you walked into the room this morning."

Tears welled as his hateful words hit their target. He might say they didn't know each other, but he knew her well enough to know where to strike. And he was right. She was guilty. Back home, she'd be wearing a red *S* for *slut* on her chest; here in Atlanta, she just wore it on her heart.

Yes, she had slept with a man she didn't know, a married man. It didn't matter that she'd thought they'd have more time, that when they'd awakened they would share last names and life stories and likes and dislikes. It didn't matter. She'd done what she'd done.

Like waking up through a fog, Cailin's mind cleared, the pain drifted away, and she once again embraced the numbness that had protected her last night. This was better, easier. This she could survive. The other—

No, she'd survive that too. She'd proved it already; she would again.

She wouldn't give him the satisfaction of seeing his words hit their mark. Instead she blanked her face, squared her shoulders decisively, and stared him down. *No matter what you've done, it doesn't mean you have to take his crap about it.*

"I know what I did, and I know what I won't do again." Why would he even want to, anyway, when he had such a beautiful wife in his bed every night?

She mentally slapped a bandage over the part of her that felt like it was bleeding out on the floor. It was time to get out those balls that had gotten her through her divorce, that had gotten her into that little black dress... Jeez, they'd gotten her into this, hadn't they? She almost fell out of her chair at that realization.

Well, the least they could do was get her out of it. "Look, we've got to work together, so it's—"

"Not necessarily."

Time stretched out as she struggled to comprehend his words. "What?"

"It might be better for both of us if you were transferred to another office."

"Transfer?" Was she supposed to be thankful the jerk wasn't firing her instead? Oh no, he wasn't pulling that card on her. "You're the senior vice president, Alex. Since the president is in California, there is no one higher than you here in Atlanta. Any transfer would be, essentially, a demotion."

She would not give an inch. Did she want to work for him? No. But she wouldn't accept a cut in rank or pay because he had chosen to deceive her. Besides, she needed this job. She had no family or friends who would acknowledge her to fall back on. The divorce had depleted her savings. She'd already started over once in the last year; she wasn't about to do it again, even to get away from this whole mess.

If he could play hardball, so could she. She firmed her voice before continuing.

"Alex, I don't care what you do outside these walls. You're free to ball the entire female population of Fulton County for all I freaking care. But if you try to remove me from this position, I will make sure everyone in this company knows what you did. Now somehow I don't think that's what you want, is it?"

Alex's face was granite hard, unyielding. "Damn it, no."

That's what I thought. Wouldn't want Mrs. Brannigan having to deal with that. She shook her head at the venom of that thought. Whether she could actually follow through with the threat, she hoped she'd never know. Cailin didn't want Sara Beth to have to deal with it either.

And, some tiny, treacherous part of her whispered, you'd still see him, even if he's not yours.

She closed the thought off and faced Alex with her shoulders squared. "I—"

The door behind her swung open, and Alex snapped, "Yes, Tammy."

The receptionist ignored his tone and rushed into speech. "Mr. Brannigan, I was trying to reach you, but no one was answering." She looked at Cailin askance. Great, now she'd earned an *L* for *lazy* to go along with her *S* for *slut*. Lovely. Before long she'd have a whole alphabet to display. "Miller in Development says they've got an emergency and he's fixin' to pull out what little of his hair is still left if you don't get down there straightaway."

Alex grunted. "Where's Ian?"

"Mr. Walker is out for a personal day."

Alex nodded. "I'll go immediately." When Tammy had departed, he zeroed in on Cailin, branding her with a look. "We'll finish this when I get back."

Not if I can help it, she thought as she watched him head out the door.

Chapter Four

"Open up, Cailin!"

She sat leaning her back against her front door, the stained-glass inset just over her head, so she didn't have to see Alex's shadow. The close call to make it out of the office before he returned from the meeting had pumped adrenaline into her blood, and now she hid, heart pounding, shocked that he'd followed her home. Why go to all that trouble for a one-night stand—a one-night stand he'd cheated on his wife with, at that?

"Cailin, your car is in the driveway. I know you're home. Open the door so we can talk."

Again? No, thank you. She'd had enough talking today. Enough for several todays, as a matter of fact. A frozen still of his face right before he told her exactly what kind of woman she was had branded itself into her brain.

Yeah, if we don't talk again, ever, I'll be perfectly happy, she thought as she pressed the heels of her hands into her eye sockets.

Keep telling yourself that, girlie. Seems there's more than one liar in this whole scenario. Not to mention, it won't be easy to manage considering you are the man's executive assistant.

She wrapped her arms around her ducked head and tried to close out the voices, both the one from outside and the one in her head.

"Cailin, I'm sorry, okay? Please open the door."

He sounded so much like Sean that tears gathered in her eyes. What was it with her and men who just wanted her when it was convenient, then

49

wanted her to disappear? *Open the door. Go away. Do what I tell you. Don't touch me. I want you. I don't want you.* She had become a yo-yo on a string, just waiting for the moment it would snap. Praying for it to snap. But instead all she got was the back-and-forth.

No more.

She'd learned the power of silence from an expert; Sean had wielded the weapon like a master, and now it was the only thing that could save her. So she waited.

An actual growl escaped Alex's mouth as he pounded on the door once more. She could hear the rumble through the solid wood and glass that shook against her back. Could he see her shadow? Did he know how close she was to him? How close she was to caving?

She squeezed her eyelids shut tight. That's what she hated more than anything: the traitorous part of her that remembered his touch, his breath, his words. The part that wanted desperately to say to heck with his marriage, his wife, everything, just let him love her, and if he couldn't love her, touch would be enough. This terrible, painful, ugly part of her she'd never known existed had sprouted like Jack's bean stalk overnight—or in an afternoon—and nothing she'd tried so far had cut it completely down.

But she'd manage. Time would do the job. *I am not an adulteress.* She would not hurt Sara Beth Brannigan that way. She stiffened her muscles and her resolve.

Alex could go to hell.

The sound of something solid bumping the glass above her head had her jerking to look. The imprint of Alex's forehead rolling back and forth arrested her breathing. His words were low, lost. "Talk to me, Cailin."

No. God, no.

As she watched, Alex turned and put his back to the door, sliding down to mirror her earlier position. His head was just visible above the bottom of the glass, and she could see he'd turned to the side so part of his face rested against a yellow rose. His words came through the door clearly.

"I'm sorry for the way I spoke to you this morning. I am, I swear. I was…angry. I lashed out at you when it was really the situation I was mad at."

Me too. But you were still a jerk.

She startled when he seemed to read her thoughts. "I was a jerk. It won't happen again."

Cailin wrapped her arms back around herself, then firmed her trembling lips and raised her chin as if he could see her. *No, it definitely won't. I'll be stronger tomorrow.* Her defiance wavered. *Just…leave me alone tonight. Please. Let me wallow like the idiot I am.*

"I wish I could make you understand. What I wanted. Why I did…what I did. There's so much I wish I could say."

Then why don't you? I felt…thought…a lot of things. None of them were real. I thought you were a jerk, but something's not right about that either. So what is going on, Alex?

"But that's not going to happen, is it?"

Why not?

"Okay," he said, as if coming to some conclusion. His next words were firm, resolved. "Thank you, Cailin. As much as you must hate me"— his breath huffed out in a rush, and she saw a hand scruff his hair—"thank you. You gave me something

51

I'll always treasure. No, not that," he said teasingly, a little bit of the old Alex sneaking through their mutual tension. He sobered immediately. "Freedom. You gave me freedom, just for a little while. Repaying you this way seems doubly unfair, but…thank you."

She shook her head in confusion.

"This isn't really helping, is it?" Alex stood up on the other side of the door and turned to face her. She wished she could see his face clearly, wished… Yeah, they'd been over all of that, hadn't they? Wishing didn't change what was.

And then his soft, damning whisper. "As much of a bastard as it makes me, I hope you don't forget what we had, even if we never have it again." The traitorous part of her latched on to that *if*, but she ignored it and watched in fascination as his hand pressed to the clear glass. "I know I won't."

Cailin clamped both hands over her mouth as the urge to respond overwhelmed her. The only choice she really had was to ignore him. Anything else would damn her soul, and not because a church or deity decreed it. Because marriage vows were sacred; "to have and to hold" actually meant something to her.

No one had understood when she'd walked away from Sean. She had forsaken her marriage vows, they'd said. But she hadn't. She'd walked away because of those vows. Because her husband had broken those vows by turning his back on her, refusing to touch her, love her, support her. Be a friend, much less a husband, to her. Alex had done the same to Sara Beth. How could she trust, much less want a man like that?

She couldn't. Wouldn't. Better to cut the cord now.

She didn't move. Not when his palm slid down the glass like a tear. Not when his footsteps retreated across the front porch. And, God help her, not even when she heard his car start, then drive away. She stayed against the door, holding herself, rocking and praying she could somehow, someway, make it through this with a vague semblance of her sanity still intact. It was a stretch, but they did say God was merciful.

You never know. Even a woman with as many letters on her chest as you might have a chance, Cailin.

∞

He was laid out across his bed when Sara Beth found him later that night. Dressed in her usual cotton cami and pajama pants, she crossed the room with her customary unhurried, feminine swing that drew every male eye that witnessed it, climbed onto the high bed, and cuddled up to his side. Her head automatically settled in the hollow of his biceps, just below his shoulder like it had a million times before, just as they'd lain together like this a million times before. So long that Alex couldn't remember anymore the first time it had happened.

"You are brooding." A mischievous spark added twinkle to her tired eyes. She was carrying a lot of weight on her shoulders supervising Ian's project and the rest of the development department, but he hadn't noticed she was tired until now. Why hadn't he? He sighed as his gaze traced a bruise-like shadow under one moss-green eye. Because he'd been too focused on his own problems, of course. Selfish bastard.

It took a moment to remember her comment. "Hmm. What makes you say that?"

She nodded toward the stereo, the sound of an acoustic guitar and Johnny Rzeznik spilling out softly. "You always listen to the Goo Goo Dolls when you're brooding. It's the only time you'll ignore how old this stuff makes you."

He poked her in the side, earning a giggle. "I'm only a couple of years older than you, love. And good music never goes out of style. I like 'this stuff,' thank you very much."

Her pert nose wrinkled. "You would."

They fell back into silence, their breathing in sync, their bodies relaxed. They'd been friends so long words weren't really necessary anymore, and yet he still felt as if she read him like an open book.

Alex shut his eyes and let the crooning music and Sara Beth's warmth along his side work their magic. These were his favorite times, in the quiet with her. They were the only times when worry and stress could be pushed away.

Except with Cailin. You weren't stressed with her either.

"Are you going to tell me what happened, Alex?"

Now that the moment was here, he found he didn't really want to; it felt like betraying Cailin. Not to mention revealing what an idiot he'd been tonight to follow her home. Instead he traced that shadow once more. "You're not getting enough sleep."

A raised brow challenged him. "That's what you're going with, really? Because I could think of much better distractions. That one isn't going to work." Sneaky fingers grabbed the T-shirt-covered skin along his ribs, almost exactly the place where he'd poked her, but the quick, vicious pinch they gave made him yelp.

A satisfied smile curved her lips. "Serves you right. Now spill it, or there's more where that came from."

"And everybody thinks you're such a lady."

Words weren't necessary. Her finger and thumb tapped together twice, hovering in the space between them.

He rubbed the offended—and now threatened—spot and tried like hell to figure out what to say.

"I know it has something to do with your new assistant."

Alex tightened his lips to keep from speaking.

"So, what, you want to get in her pants? Of course you do. I've been around you too long to miss *that* look in your eye."

Sara Beth laughed when all he could get out was spluttered gibberish. Heat rose to embarrass him. "God, woman, you're a menace."

She propped her head up on one hand and giggled over his arm at him. "I know, love." A pause. "So...is that it?"

"Not exactly." Sensing tension and something else he couldn't quite put his finger on creeping into her still form, reaching across the inches separating them, he gathered his shrinking balls from their hiding place and forced out the words. "We...were together. This past weekend."

Nothing. Just quiet breathing, then finally, "Together?"

"I went to Thrice, remember?" It made him a coward, but he threw an arm over his eyes, desperate to avoid hers. This was new ground for them, and he had no idea how she'd take it.

"So you met, danced…"

"And had sex."

"Good."

He jerked upright. "What?" He couldn't have heard that right.

"I said, 'good.' You needed it." Sara Beth sat up too, reaching out to grip his jaw and tug it toward her; his nose ended up inches from hers. "You think I'm stupid? I knew this would happen eventually." She searched his soul through his irises, and a crease appeared between her eyebrows. "Didn't you?"

"Sara Beth, you deserve—"

"I've gotten way more than I ever deserved in you, love. Don't doubt that I know that, all the way." She gave him a quick kiss on the tip of his nose before releasing him. "So you went to bed with her; that's kinda awkward now that you know she works for you."

"Not nearly as awkward as her thinking I'm an adulterer who deserves to be castrated."

Sara Beth winced. Then her irrepressible smile returned. "Now wouldn't that be a loss to the human race."

Drawing one knee up between them, she laid her head on it, staring at him. Waiting. Fuck, she knew him too well.

"I tried to talk to her about everything. I didn't… Let's just say I made things worse." Major understatement. He'd spent the last nine hours wishing his control had been stronger than the pendulum swing of emotions that had ridden him for those few brief minutes in his office this morning.

"Got mad, huh?"

"Yes, *love*"—he used the pet name deliberately, knowing she'd hear the *minx* it actually meant—"very mad."

"It hurt, having her see you that way." Her fingers tapped out a thoughtful rhythm on her kneecap. "She means something to you."

Alex shook his head at that last statement. "Her opinion of me matters, more than I realized." *More than anything, maybe.*

Which made his failure doubly damning. Stern and tough had been his aim—keep the feelings locked down tight; they wouldn't help anyway. Then he'd looked at her tear-swollen face and felt helpless, torn between his need to comfort her and the need to keep his word to Sara Beth. He hadn't known what to say—that had been the absolute truth. The pain her reaction generated had surprised him and blown the gasket off his anger.

Could he be any more of a pussy? He wanted to make it up to her; he wanted her out of here; he didn't know what he wanted.

"So what's the plan?"

"For what?" he asked.

"For winning her over."

He ran his hand back and forth across his chest, the rasp of the T-shirt against his skin a dim reflection of the grim resignation scouring his mind. "No plan."

"What? Why? Alex—"

Gently shaking his head at her, he pointed out, "There is no win-win solution here. If I'm with her and someone finds out... It can't happen. And what kind of offer is that? 'Hey, let's fuck. But you can't tell anyone. And you can't be seen with me in public. Oh, and by the way, I'm not really a prick for sleeping around on my wife, but I can't tell you why.'"

"Alex—"

"No! We've talked about this. I will not jeopardize you. He cannot know."

Sara Beth shivered, and he gathered her back into his arms, resting his chin on the top of her head, surrounding her with his strength. His priorities had been set years ago, long before their six-month-old marriage, and loneliness or horniness or whatever this was wouldn't change them. He loved Sara Beth too much to even consider it.

Several minutes passed before she stirred. "Do you regret it?" she asked him softly.

Alex pulled back to stare straight into her eyes. Brushing her long ginger-red bangs away from her face, he brushed his lips just as tenderly along the corner of her mouth, the same spot as this morning, the spot where he always kissed her. His spot. "Not for a moment, love. Not for a moment."

Forcing himself to walk away from Cailin tonight had felt like a kick to his gut, but he'd known it was necessary. He wasn't free to have her, not now, possibly not ever, and she deserved better than the self-serving asshole he would be if he allowed himself to take her again. How they'd both make it through the next months, he wasn't sure, but one thing was certain: if he'd thought his life had been a hard, private hell before, he hadn't seen anything yet.

Chapter Five

"Mr. Keane on line one, Mr. Brannigan."

Alex gritted his teeth. After being subjected to it for the past two weeks, Cailin's clinical tone irritated him almost as much as the knowledge that he'd have to talk to Sara Beth's father. It wasn't like he could get out of it; the man was CEO of Keane Industries. Sometimes it seemed he existed just to make their lives a living hell. There was a time when Alex had respected him tremendously, back before he had seen how John Keane treated his daughter, but that respect had come and gone a long time ago.

Clicking his Bluetooth to the correct channel, he braced himself to be pleasant. "John! How's sunny California?"

He thought he'd miss California when they moved here to Atlanta, especially the milder weather, but Alex would have gladly given up the next six years of sunny-and-seventy days to get Sara Beth away from her father's constant interference—which was, in effect, what he'd done, wasn't it?

"Alex." That stern tone still had the power to draw starch into his spine. Old habits. "What's going on with this problem in development? Can't that Walker idiot get his head out of his ass? I sent you out there to fix things, not let that fellow float into the exosphere and make them worse."

As if Alex could really control Ian, not that it was his job. The man was fast becoming the most recognized researcher in the field of augmented-reality applications, essentially the use of overlay displays on real-time pictures to "augment" or enhance what a viewer was seeing, and he worked much better without interference. Sara Beth understood that, and her running of the development department had freed Ian to focus on his research, as well as giving her a position of power within the company. Eventually, they hoped, that power could be garnered into influence on the board and disarm John's threats to cut her out of the company now that her husband was in charge. "I'm waiting on Sara Beth and Ian for an update now."

John humphed. "Don't have time for you to be sitting on your hands, young man, especially not waiting on a woman. We need results. This research has been six years in the making—"

Ignoring the dig at Sara Beth, Alex said, "And will handle six more minutes, John. Relax."

Alex could practically feel the blood beginning to boil in the man's veins through the phone line, but John's only response was a grunt.

Might as well get it over with; John was never in this bad a mood unless he'd had words with Sara Beth. "Is it just me today, or is there something else bothering you?"

"Usually it is you," the other man grumbled. They'd known each other long enough for John to use him as a scapegoat for his ill humor and for Alex to mostly let it slide right off his back. Mostly. "Sara Elizabeth called."

Damn. "Really?"

"Yes. The girl still doesn't have her head on right." The man never called her by her preferred name, and he never called her a woman. She would always be a girl in his eyes, which Alex could understand to some extent. Sara Beth's mother had died when she was a baby, so she was the only family the man had left. But she'd grown up a long time ago.

"Careful, John." Alex drawled the warning softly.

"Truth, Alex. She says she's still not pregnant."

A crick in his neck sent a sharp pain across his shoulders. He and Sara Beth had fallen asleep cuddled together, and by the time he'd woken up, his arm had been numb and his neck was killing him. The sudden tensing of his muscles set it off again. "We haven't been married that long. Sara Beth has her career. Give it time."

"She doesn't need a career; that's what she has you for. And I have given it time. Six months. That is plenty of time for you two to start on a grandchild. It's expected. The Keane line must go on." A heavy sigh sounded through Alex's Bluetooth. If it weren't for the hurt John inflicted on Sara Beth on an almost daily basis, Alex would have felt sorry for the man. Someone that rigid had to find life painful, unless they had the ability to make life accommodate them. Which John did, for the most part. Sara Beth had accommodated him as much as she was able, but not in this. "Hell, you even had eighteen damn months of the engagement to get her pregnant. I'd have accepted a little scandal if it meant the line was secure, but here we are and no bun in the oven. You don't have any problems I should know about, do you, boy?"

Alex counted very slowly to ten before responding. "I've told you I won't discuss this with you, John. It will happen when it happens. When Sara Beth is ready. There is still plenty of time."

"Like hell there is. I haven't worked my whole life just to have this company flushed down the tubes because my daughter isn't *ready* to do her familial duty. She needs to—"

"Enough!" Fortunately Ian Walker chose that moment to push casually through Alex's office door, hands full of a laptop and various files and papers seemingly ready to escape at any moment. Sara Beth followed, looking cool and confident despite whatever words she'd had with her father that morning. Alex breathed a silent *thank you, Lord* and stood to grab Ian's load before it toppled to the floor. "Here they are now. Let me switch you to the conference line."

"How are you this morning, John?" Ian greeted his boss as soon as the speakerphone came on. "Good, I hope."

"Still breathing," John said.

Ian just chuckled, his easygoing nature front and center as usual. "Well, that's got to count for something, right? The alternative is much worse."

"John," Sara Beth said. She never called him *Dad* or *Father* at work. Despite the fact that he didn't take her seriously, Sara Beth hadn't trained for years to run this company only to allow her father to undermine her abilities or her authority. Pride swelled in Alex's chest as he considered the strides she'd made since moving to Atlanta and taking over Ian's department.

"Sara Elizabeth." John's impatience soaked the words. "Thought you had things to do this morning."

"I do. It's called work."

John grunted his opinion of that. "Can we just get on with it, please?"

Ian brought them up to speed on the final stages of the research he was conducting—a project that would ultimately make AR affordably available in every car windshield, phone or camera view screen, pair of glasses, and possibly even contacts for the rapidly growing consumer public. Alex listened impatiently as John fawned over Ian's progress, then fought Sara Beth's every comment as they hammered out the details on the presentation of said research at an international consortium in a couple of months. By the time he was ready to reach through the phone and strangle his father-in-law, lunchtime had rolled around. Alex thankfully pushed the button to cut their connection to the LA office. He rubbed his grainy eyes, then turned a jaundiced one on Ian's trademark chuckle.

"So, was it just me, or was the old man in rare form this morning?" Ian asked with a knowing look.

Sara Beth gave a delicate snort, the sound strangely reminiscent of her father's own displeasured grunts. "Isn't he always?"

"Of course," Ian said. Then, taking advantage of the friendship they'd formed since Alex and Sara Beth had moved to Atlanta, he asked, "Problems on the home front?"

"Not ours," Alex countered before Sara Beth could respond. "Just his. Obviously." When was it ever anything else?

Ian shrugged. "Educated guess. You both look like you haven't slept in a week." He tipped his head to one side. "Make that two." A nod indicated the phone on the table between them. "Still pushing the baby-factory line?"

"God, yes." Sara Beth sighed. "Excuse me a moment, won't you?" She stood, her posture at once weary, and crossed to close herself in the private bathroom off Alex's office.

Alex watched her, worry surfacing. Her fatigue was obvious, but he had a feeling it wasn't physical. Dropping to a quieter tone, he told Ian, "I thought moving here would help, but…"

"Nope," Ian teased, trying to ease the strain in his own way, Alex knew. "Guess you better get busy then, man." He gathered his papers in a haphazard pile on top of his computer. "I'm just thankful you're not still available. Leaves the field open for the rest of us."

"Oh?"

"Yeah." His gaze strayed to the office door, and he licked his lips. "So what's the deal with your new secretary?"

"Executive assistant," Alex corrected absently, not liking the look on the other man's face. "Why?"

"Why? 'Cause she's seriously hot, in case you hadn't noticed, Mr. Happily Married."

Alex could have been dead and still noticed, but he didn't tell his friend that. The growl that threatened to erupt at Ian's expression was harder to hold back. He rubbed a hand down his face. He seriously had to get his shit together.

He hadn't lied to Sara Beth the other night; he would never regret marrying her. It was keeping their secret that created this vampiric drain on him. That, and not handling things better than he was. He was supposed to be the strong one, the protector. He'd never appreciated how relaxing it was to just be himself until that was no longer an option. Sara Beth had been forced to pretend her whole life, and though he couldn't stop that—yet—he wanted her life to be as carefree as he could make it until their farce could come to an end. Instead he was obsessed with a certain sweet blonde and doing a shitty job at protecting anyone, especially his wife.

Ignoring Ian's comment, he turned toward the door. Intent on staying as far from this conversation as possible, he didn't hear Cailin on the other side until they collided as he rounded the opening.

"Whoa!" Cailin brought her hands up automatically, and the feel of them slapping onto his chest brought instantaneous pleasure that stole his breath, along with every thought in his head. A nearly silent groan escaped, and he knew she heard him, because her eyelids lowered to half-mast and her heavy inhale rang in his ears.

Of course, it could have been the impact, but the way her body melted into him seemed more like instinct.

His instinct had kicked in as well at the feel of her hips in his hands. He pulled her closer, aligning their bodies so her soft mound met the hardened shaft making its insistent presence known. They fit perfectly, more perfectly than any woman he'd ever held against him except Sara Beth, and she'd never drawn a sexual response from him. It was as if his body had known from the beginning that she was destined for someone else and hadn't wanted to tangle him up in a hopeless situation.

So what are you thinking now, dickhead?

"Alex," she whispered, her voice a tantalizing elixir that drew his attention to her mouth. White, even teeth bit down on her plump lower lip, and as if in a dream, he leaned down and nuzzled her lip away before licking the abused flesh tenderly.

Pressure against his heart snapped him out of his daze. "Don't," she whispered, taking a step back.

His grip tightened instinctively before he released her. He stood for a moment, his gaze transfixed on her mouth. When he raised his eyes, the sight of tears glistening in hers was like a mule kick to the gut. *Shitty job, indeed.* He cleared his throat and shook his head, struggling to clear it as well. "Um, lunch."

Cailin clasped her hands in front of her stomach. Was his warmth still there? Did she want to hold on to it as long as she could, the way he did?

"I was just coming to tell you it should be here in about five minutes," she told him.

A sharp jerk of his head acknowledged her words, and she turned hastily away. Alex stared after her longer than he should, then returned to his office door, but couldn't resist a last look back at her retreating figure. When he finally entered his office, Sara Beth was there, amusement lighting her eyes.

Proving she'd heard his and Ian's conversation despite their low tones, she said, "Yeah, you noticed." With a wink, she patted him on the chest and moved toward the door. "Enjoy your lunch. I have a date."

A quick glance at Ian revealed even more laughter at Alex's expense. "Just be happy she's not the jealous type," the man said with a nod toward Sara Beth's departing back. "Little or not, she can still kick your ass."

Alex balled his hands into tight fists and planted his feet hard, fighting the overwhelming urge to lodge one or the other right in his friend's cocky jaw.

Damn.

∞

The minute the elevator doors closed behind Cailin, she jammed the side of her hand into her mouth and bit down hard. She wouldn't scream; she wouldn't. That would bring every self-respecting employee for miles, and then she'd have to explain why the heck she'd screamed in the elevator for no obvious reason. It would be better if the elevator just dropped her to her death right here and now.

When she got home, then she'd scream. She would turn on a nice, hot—scalding hot—shower, get naked, and get rid of her anxieties all at once. It was the perfect solution, assuming she could hold on that long. And that the neighbors didn't call the cops. Now that would be embarrassing.

Elevator. Drop. Please.

They could always assume you were having hot, screaming sex.

Didn't she wish.

No, she didn't, because the truth was—the truth she'd awakened to just an hour or so ago—she couldn't imagine having hot, screaming sex with anyone but Alex. Married Alex. Two-timing Alex, as contrary as that seemed to what she'd viewed of his character the past two weeks. The Alex she was drawn to, the one with veracity, with a command and compassion totally at odds with who she knew him to truly be.

From the moment she listened to him walk away that night at her house, she'd been living in a fog, a haze that surrounded her, insulated her, made work and living and breathing bearable. Even the realization that she would divorce Sean had not been so difficult to accept. Maybe because she had done something completely abhorrent to her, however unwittingly: she'd had sex with a married man.

Or maybe it stemmed from her confusion about Alex. She'd watched him carefully over the past fourteen days; one thing she would never have pegged him as was an adulterer. He conducted the business of Keane Industries with precision and consistency and attention to detail. He treated employees and customers with courtesy, yet stood firm against anyone who did not do the same. She would have sworn on a stack of Bibles a mile high that the man she worked for embodied honor and integrity and loyalty.

Yet she knew for a fact that he was not faithful.

His deception was flawless, even with Sara Beth. The woman was in the office constantly, dropping in for lunch, just to chat, as well as frequently consulting Alex on business matters. Cailin witnessed them together often, and not a single crack in Alex's facade indicated he felt anything but totally content with Sara Beth. They were so close that it seemed at times they communicated with their own language, on a wavelength 100 percent separate from the rest of the world. They genuinely loved each other. How could a man who loved like that generate such a deep emotional connection in another woman? Deep enough that Cailin was very much afraid she could easily care about him.

But not love. Please, dear Lord, not love.

Numbness had protected her when the confusion and chaos and pain became too much. But Alex's touch today had brought her back to life, like

Sleeping Beauty awakening from her frozen sleep. Only she wanted desperately to go back. Being awake hurt too much.

Shaking out her throbbing hand, she stepped off the elevator and into the lobby. Muggy heat hit her in the face when she opened the lobby door and headed down the street. A round of errands would keep her out of the office for a little while; thank goodness Mondays were her designated gofer days. The last time she did this, she'd been trying to decipher Alex's detailed instructions, the various brands he needed, finding the locations of the shops. Today would have been smoother had she not been shaking from his touch, from the tenderness in his eyes that confused her all the more.

By the time she made it to her last stop, Beaker's, her strength was zapped and droplets of sweat trickled in rivulets from under her thick hair. She juggled Alex's dry cleaning around so she could reach into her purse and grab a clip, jamming it into a quick twist at the back of her head to get the weight of the heavy curls off her neck. The relief as she walked into the cooler shade of the sandwich shop hit instantly.

Beaker's Deli was a popular lunch destination for the offices in the vicinity, including theirs, but at two o'clock, the crowds had thinned enough for her to grab a quick bite. Even so, by the time she'd placed her order, Cailin's arms ached. She carried everything to a chair at a table by the front window, then returned to fill her drink cup and pick up her tray. The Caesar chicken wrap sparked her taste buds with the first bite, and she found herself eating hungrily for the first time in days. Nothing tasted good with a side dish of depression; at least the return of emotion meant her palate could also return to normal. Hey, if sex was off the menu, good food could make up for it. And she'd prove it tonight with a pint of rocky-road ice cream.

Sipping her sweet tea and people watching allowed for a few extra minutes to gather her strength—and courage—for the return trip. Hopefully Alex would still be involved with Ian when she got back.

Ian, the office flirt. The man might head the biggest and most lucrative research project at Keane Industries, which meant he was brilliant, but from all appearances there was not a serious bone in his body. He'd flirted outrageously when he came in the office this morning, then even worse when she brought their lunch, to the point where her tongue had felt tied in permanent knots. Alex's dark stare and the memory of that almost kiss had unnerved her enough; she certainly didn't need to add another, albeit very attractive, man's attention to the mix.

A feminine giggle caught her attention as she took a final bite of her wrap. She shifted, her gaze wandering the café, and noticed a table in a rear corner, the chairs turned so their backs faced her. The occupants, two women, laughed and chatted together. Something about one of the women was familiar, but it wasn't until the woman turned her head that Cailin realized it was Sara Beth.

Look away, she thought. Yet taking her eyes off the woman proved impossible.

Bold red hair lay like a curtain around her delicate features, her bangs ultralong in front and trimmed short on her neck in back. When she twisted a bit more toward her companion, her face came clearly into view. Beauty shone from her dark green eyes and perfect bow lips, and Cailin knew from seeing Sara Beth around the office and hearing others speak about her that the daughter of the company's CEO was beautiful inside as well as out. The woman's build was small, almost pixielike, the perfect foil for Alex's dark, muscular good looks. Everything Cailin had always wanted to be. Her failure to keep Sean happy, her inability to have a baby weighed heavily on her as she watched the woman eat and talk. Sara Beth seemed to have it all.

Trying to shake off the thought—and the self-pity it generated—Cailin turned her attention to the other woman at the table. Taller, darker, with olive skin and nut-brown hair and eyes. It took Cailin a moment to place her as one of the women she'd seen when she went through processing with the human resources department on her first day. Samantha, maybe? Something like that. Her first day at Keane Industries remained a huge blur in her mind, everything overshadowed by the discovery of Alex's marriage and her own duplicity in his deceit.

She'd welcomed that blur for two weeks. But today...today woke her up fast. Guilt slammed into her. God, she'd frozen completely at his touch, the feel of him just so darn good. She'd wanted his hands everywhere, his tongue in her mouth. He'd been hard against her. Amazing. Appalling. How could she feel this way about a man without integrity? Without honor? He was worse than Sean, wasn't he? At least Sean hadn't turned to another woman; Alex had.

Her gaze lingered on Sara Beth and her companion. The woman lifted a fry and placed it in Sara Beth's mouth, and the look they exchanged...

Cailin frowned. Something about it just... She didn't know.

She shook her head as if the rattling would straighten out her thoughts, her confusion. Heck, maybe even her life. But experience had taught her pain didn't heal that fast. She had a long road ahead of her.

And a long afternoon, she thought as she looked over at the pile of stuff she still had to schlep back to the office. She'd better get on it.

Cailin hurried to take care of her trash. Just as she settled her tray on the waiting shelf, she heard her name being called in the feminine voice she'd most wanted to avoid.

"It's great to see you here," Sara Beth cried with what seemed like genuine excitement as Cailin cautiously approached their table. "Sam, this is Alex's new executive assistant, Cailin. Cailin, Sam."

Cailin smiled a hello, but Sara Beth was far from done.

"Sit, please." That gentle addition didn't change the command of the first word. Sara Beth patted the chair kitty-corner to hers. "How have things been going?"

"Busy."

"It's always busy when Alex is involved," Sara Beth said with a grin.

Sam laughed. "He has a reputation to uphold, you know."

Cailin felt a little out of the loop but forced herself to relax. More than likely the feeling grew from her uneasiness around Sara Beth. Somehow every time she saw the woman, those imagined letters sewn into her chest began to ache as if in recognition, and the urge to confess threatened to overwhelm her. But she got the feeling Sara Beth didn't need to know her sins any more than Cailin wanted to share them.

"So do you live around here?" Sam asked, pulling Cailin out of her reverie.

"Actually I'm new to Atlanta. It feels small-town outside of the business districts, even though it's not, really. Took a little getting used to, but I like it."

"I feel the same way," Sara Beth said. "Alex and I moved here about six months ago when Dad agreed to transfer us from California. The weather's definitely taken some getting used to."

Sam chuckled. "Definitely. I don't think I've ever seen you wear your hair this short, and June hasn't even arrived yet."

"So you two knew each other before?" Cailin looked from one to the other and couldn't miss the long look that passed between them.

"Sam was transferred too. Several of the LA employees were moved out when the office first opened."

Cailin nodded. "Well, just a warning: summers here in the South are a bit like pea soup—thick and very humid. Invest in cool clothes." She cocked her head and smiled. "And warm ones. We might get snow this winter. It happens every once in a while."

The two women looked at her with varying degrees of dismay.

"You'll like it, really," she reassured them.

"So you're from the South, then?" Sara Beth asked.

"Born and bred."

"Are you here alone? No significant other?" Sam asked.

Cailin ducked her head, but not before seeing Sara Beth elbow her companion lightly in the ribs. The accompanying scowl was almost comical, it was so ferocious. "Um, I'm recently divorced."

True sympathy colored Sam's voice. "I'm sorry."

Cailin shrugged and gathered her purse. "It's fine, believe me. And now, I have to get a move on. Alex is waiting."

Sara Beth sent her a wide smile. "The longer he waits, the more appreciative he is. Trust me."

Again that feeling that she'd missed something passed through her, but Cailin brushed it away. A few minutes later she stepped back into the sunshine, lugging Alex's dry cleaning once more.

Chapter Six

What the heck was I thinking? Cailin asked herself as she climbed onto a padded bar stool on the shadowed end of the bar at Thrice. Friday night hopped—or thrashed, depending on which corner you looked at. Various enclaves had developed in different areas of the room: headbangers, goths, twentysomethings… You name it, Thrice had it going on. The wild feel to the air rankled her nerves, already shot at this, her second trip to the nightclub. She'd met Alex here a month ago; surely she could meet someone else, anyone else. She had to get him out of her head.

"What can I get you, beautiful?"

The bartender leaned across the wide expanse of the gleaming bar toward her. The tag on his shirt said *Brad*. When she met his eyes, a glittering smile told her he was a charmer she would want to keep an eye out for.

Tongue-tied, Cailin found her answer caught somewhere between her head and her brain. She could count on two fingers the amount of times she'd ordered an alcoholic drink in her adult life. It's not like there was a menu! What the heck should she order when she didn't know for sure what anything was called, or what was in it, for that matter?

"Um…" She bit down on her lower lip in an effort to curb her embarrassment.

Brad seemed to sense her dilemma. "Not much of a drinker then, huh, beautiful?"

Cailin shook her head, figuring that was plenty of response with the pounding drums blaring from the stage below.

"Okay," he answered, "let's play twenty questions. But don't worry," he assured her as her eyes widened, "there's really only two. Okay, maybe three."

Cailin nodded.

Brad's laugh was deep and throaty, sexy, and yet not so much as a tingle went through her. On an aesthetic level, she could see the appeal, but her body wasn't getting the message. *Doesn't mean it won't, girl. Just give yourself a chance.*

"So, first question: Sweet or bitter?" At her obvious confusion, he clarified. "Do you like your drinks bitter or sweet?"

"Sweet."

He jerked a nod. "Good." Making a show of considering his next question, even going so far as to tap his chin with a long forefinger until she laughed, he finally asked, "Frozen or on the rocks?"

Cailin was getting the hang of this game. "Frozen."

"Hot damn, we're on a roll!" Brad slapped his palms together and rubbed them vigorously. "Let's see…strawberry or coconut?"

That one was harder. "Hmm. I like both, but let's go with strawberry."

"Okay, how about a frozen strawberry margarita? Good staple. Can't go wrong with it."

Cailin agreed. "Sounds good. Thank you."

"No problem—" He lifted a brow in inquiry.

"Cailin."

Brad reached across to shake her hand politely. "Nice to meet you, Cailin." He tapped his name tag. "Guess what my name is?"

"Would I win the game then?" she asked with a laugh.

"You've already won our game, beautiful."

Brad shot her a seductive smile that should've sent the temperature in the room soaring several degrees, then turned to start on her drink.

Cailin went back to people watching. As much as she enjoyed interacting with others—when they carried the conversation, of course—she was always more comfortable on the outside looking in. It was easier watching than trying to figure out how to actually do, how to get involved with people and not become mired in their expectations and rules and just plain crap sometimes. Part of the reason she'd been with Sean as long as she had was because she was so used to the outsider role that she hadn't really recognized that she'd ended up there, in her marriage of all places. She'd been so used to being lonely that it hadn't rung any alarm bells when it crept between her and Sean, hadn't alerted her to her husband's slow defection until it was too late.

It was funny when she bothered to think about it, really—funny sad, not funny ha-ha. She had ended up in the same position with Alex, hadn't she? On the outside looking in. If she could ignore what was on the inside, it might be easier to bear, but how could she ignore a man she was so fascinated with that not even his having a wife could cool her down for long?

Thus her trip to Thrice.

Brad returned with her drink, flirting a bit more before heading over to help with a large group that arrived all at once. Cailin sipped the frozen concoction with pleasure. And she watched. And watched.

What had made Alex choose her? She'd been on the dance floor, but she knew better than anyone that her skill in that area wouldn't be special enough to draw a man like him. She frowned, trying to piece the puzzle together. Had it been the dress? Had her clothes declared to the world *I'm desperate; pick me up?* Chemistry had certainly been a factor. For goodness's sake, look how quick they had ended up in—

"Ah, my lady returns. How are you this evening, miss?"

Cailin turned, surprised. The man behind her stood a good foot taller than her own five-three, towering over her even when he leaned one elbow on the bar. A rugged jaw tempered the boyish good looks, keeping him from being pretty; instead he drew second, third, and probably fourth looks from the women passing their spot. Cailin looked at those women, then at him, but it wasn't until he smiled and lifted a single dark brow that she realized who he was. A hot flush that had nothing to do with the alcohol in her drink swept across her neck and face.

"Oh Lord," she whispered. It was the man who'd opened the door to the office that night, the one who'd known Alex on sight, who had allowed them in with only that raised eyebrow as comment.

The man traced what must be a bright red stain across her cheeks with a cool finger. "Ah, none of that, now." Leaning in, he whispered directly in her tingling ear, "Your secret is safe with me, my lady."

Cailin turned her head, bringing them practically nose to nose. "Thank you… I'm afraid I don't—"

"Damien. Thrice's owner. And you are?"

Oh. "Cailin."

"Beautiful." It seemed to be the adjective most fitting tonight since two men had now used it on her. Cailin fought not to roll her eyes at him. "I'm a friend of Alex's from way back."

"I see."

She sat for a moment under the man's careful scrutiny, sipping her drink, with no idea what to say.

"So where is Alex tonight?" Damien asked.

She jerked her head toward him. Wrinkling her brows, she asked, "How should I know?"

"Ah, I see." Something in his face closed down, and Damien's tone froze her in place when he continued. "So it's like that."

Like what? This man had known Alex a long time, he said. Did he not know Alex was married? Or was he just covering for his friend so Alex could get some tail on the side? Cailin shook her head, confused. "Damien, Alex is—"

"Married? I know."

"I didn't."

The man's cavalier attitude hurt. Maybe she was supposed to be able to just have sex and not feel anything—that's what she'd actually been looking for that night, as a matter of fact. But even if she had been able to look at it that way, no one should take marriage that lightly.

She stared at him, hoping something in his expression would explain what she was having such a difficult time comprehending. Finally she gave up and said, "I don't—"

"Understand." Damien ignored her tightened lips at his rude interruption and continued. "I know you don't. Few people do. And no, I don't condone affairs."

Cailin plopped her elbows on the bar, dropped her head into her hands, and rubbed her temples in slow circles. Damien's low chuckle made her want to smack him, but since he owned the place, that probably wasn't a good idea. She'd seen the size of the bouncers out front, after all.

"Cailin, I'm sorry. I'm not making fun, I promise." He took one of her hands and held it in his own. "Let's just say I have a fair idea of what's going on with Alex. Although most people wouldn't understand, I do, and I won't begrudge him what little bit of happiness he can squeeze out."

"But he's happy with Sara Beth. I've seen them together." All the darn time.

Damien's eyes narrowed on her. "You know them personally," he guessed shrewdly. "Your presence here tonight isn't just some delayed craving for a one-night stand with no forwarding address."

She turned her head away. Brad stood at the back of the bar, rubbing a fluffy white towel over a series of wineglasses. Blaming the welling behind her eyes on staring at the bartender was flimsy, but it was better than Damien's pity.

"I'm sorry again, Cailin. I didn't understand the situation. I should have known—but then, I haven't spoken with Alex since the opening. Look, Alex and Sara Beth grew up together. They've been best friends longer than any of us can remember. But just because you love someone doesn't mean you are in love with them." He shook his head when she opened her mouth to speak. "I can't say more than that. I wish I could. But what I know about their situation is based on long years of trust in me as a friend. I wouldn't share what they've told me with anyone else without their permission." He hesitated a moment, and the first hint of uncertainty she'd seen crept into his eyes. "Does Alex know?"

"Know what?"

"That you're in love with him?"

Shock zinged up her spine. "I'm not—"

Damien laid a quick finger against her lips, releasing her quickly. "Never mind. I shouldn't have asked." Brad stepped close to serve a nearby customer, and Damien waited until the other man left to continue. "I wish I had some words of wisdom to give you, but I don't." His brows lowered in concern. "From the looks of things, it's already rough."

Oh God. If this man could see how torn she was about Alex, so could everyone else. What could she do—

"Stop worrying. I'm just good at reading my fellow humans. I spend a lot of time doing it." He waved a hand to indicate Thrice's crowded floor.

"I don't need anyone's pity."

"No, you don't." He stared at her a moment longer. "And offering to be here for you won't do any good either."

She shook her head. She didn't know him. For that matter, she didn't know anyone she'd share this with. Not anymore.

Damien leaned in and lowered his voice, but sincerity still bled through. "I'll offer anyway, Cailin. Because it's gonna get worse before it gets better. And for what very little it is worth, I'm sorry for that." He ran a rough hand up her cheek into her hair, hooking the curly strands behind her ear. Then he turned and walked away.

∞

Two pairs of eyes stared back from the shadows of the couch as Alex walked into the den. He resisted the urge to sigh, knowing Sara Beth would see it even in the gloom wrapping the two as they watched a movie. It wasn't that he minded Sam being here so much as he had simply hoped to sneak in without any actual human contact whatsoever. His social skills were wearing thin these days.

Bending over the two women, he tapped each on the head with a light kiss, then asked, "What are you watching?"

"Milla Jovovich, *Resident Evil*. That woman is so kick-ass."

There was no polite response that wouldn't make him sound like a sexist pig, so he didn't bother trying to find one. Nodding would have to do.

He sniffed, noting the heavy scent of oregano and tomato sauce and sausage in the air. "Any pizza left for me?"

Sam smiled up at him. "Of course. We left it in the oven to stay warm."

Alex grunted a thank-you as he peeled off his suit coat, then flopped into a nearby chair.

Sara Beth's knowing look generated a guilt he tried not to feel. "Just home from the office?" she asked him.

"Yep."

"On a Friday night?" Her brow lifted above those shame-inducing eyes.

"On a Friday night." This time the sigh escaped, watched or not. Reaching up to tug off his tie seemed like too much effort, but he did it anyway, hoping it would help him breathe.

"You didn't keep Cailin there this late." Sara Beth's statement was matter-of-fact with the slightest undercurrent of accusation.

"Of course not," he snapped.

Regret hit instantly. The truth was, he rarely got any work done when Cailin was in the office, so he resorted to staying late to catch up with all the stuff his distracted mind hadn't been focused enough to tackle during the day. He should just say that, he knew, but he couldn't. Sara Beth was the little sister he'd never had. Big brothers didn't dump their problems on their little sisters; they sheltered them, protected them. He'd spent so much time holding back things he thought might hurt Sara Beth, trying to insulate her from the pieces of their world that battered and bruised her, that stopping the pattern seemed impossible.

They were adults. She was in a committed relationship. He had agreed to the marriage of his own free will. And still, even though she already knew about Cailin, he couldn't talk about it, not tonight. He didn't want Sara Beth feeling even guiltier about his "issues" than she already was.

Another heavy sigh escaped as he leaned back and closed his eyes.

The sound of her head shaking—he could hear the back-and-forth swish of her hair—would have been lost in the noise Sam made getting up from the couch to walk into the kitchen, but Alex's lifetime of experience with Sara Beth made him sharper than most. Her voice heavy with concern, she said, "You work too hard."

He shrugged. He was being a bastard, he knew, but the last thing he wanted tonight was the third degree.

Sara Beth held her silence, though she didn't restart the paused movie.

Alex must have dozed off, because the next thing he knew, a heavy plate of warm pizza was being set in his lap. Trying to tell himself the power nap had energized instead of sapped him, he shot Sam a look of gratitude and chugged half of the cold beer she slapped into his hand. Sam gave him a warm, sympathetic smile and resumed her seat on the couch with Sara Beth.

So the minx had been talking, huh? Or was he just that obvious? It shouldn't matter that Sam knew what he'd gotten himself into; she was part of their family now. It rankled nonetheless. But if Sara Beth needed to talk things out with Sam, he'd ignore it. This once, anyway.

The topping-laden deep-dish was his favorite, the cheese hot and melty and perfect. He managed to swallow four bites before he dropped his fork onto the plate and set it on the nearby coffee table. The beer he finished off, then set the empty bottle next to his plate. The girls talked on the couch; the movie blurred in front of his eyes. His knee bounced as he fought the hole digging a tunnel deeper into his gut. Finally, unable to sit still any longer, he hopped up and gathered his dishes.

Sam and Sara Beth startled as if they'd forgotten his presence. When Sara Beth laughed, he couldn't help growling, knowing he was acting like an ass but unable to stop all the same.

Sam raised an eyebrow at the sound. "Damn, Alex, you're a little tense." Her typical sarcastic smirk made an appearance. "I think you need to get laid."

"I already did that," he snapped. Slamming out of the living room was pure defense against their shock. Embarrassment made him ignore the apology Sam called after his retreating figure.

He was banging his forehead into the cabinet next to the sink when Sara Beth followed him into the kitchen. Feeling like a teenage boy on a hormone roller coaster instead of a man in his thirties—and in control of his runaway moods—Alex shook his head against the cabinet door. "I'm sorry. I'll tell her I'm sorry too. Just...give me a minute."

Sara Beth came up behind him, her warm hands massaging the tense muscles of his back through the thin shield of his dress shirt. The touch calmed him more than anything else, even the beer he'd downed way too fast on a mostly empty stomach. That stomach tensed when Sara Beth murmured against his back, "She didn't mean it, you know." The press of her lips against his shoulder blade made him feel like a total jerk.

"I know." Just one more thing to be disappointed in himself over.

"Alex..." Sara Beth tugged him around, forcing him to face her. When he tilted his head up so he didn't have to look her in the eye, she grabbed his ears and pulled until they were nose to nose. "Talk to me."

Alex stared into her eyes, feeling lost. How did he explain what even he didn't understand? It had been a month since he'd met Cailin. That certainly wasn't long enough to be in love with her, but she was all he thought about. He watched her at work, saw her patience, her compassion, her ability to put up boundaries to protect him without offending everyone who wanted a piece of his time. She'd wormed her way into his heart—he couldn't explain it any other way. His head said he had no clue what he was feeling, but his gut...it told him something altogether different.

How did he choose between the woman he loved and the woman he wanted?

Sara Beth nodded sagely as if she could read his thoughts on his face. "It's Cailin, isn't it?"

He just closed his eyes.

She wasn't going to let him get out of this so easily. "Alex, what are you waiting for? It's obvious you want her; you've already had her. This is making you miserable," she said, obviously exasperated. "Is it me? Because you know I'm good with it. I have sex whenever I want it. I don't expect you to go without."

And that was the crux of the matter: he could have sex if that was all he wanted. Without the least amount of conceit, he knew any number of women would jump at the chance to be in his bed. But Cailin wasn't a just-sex kind of woman. "It's not that simple, and you know it. Cailin would never accept the kind of arrangement I could offer her." Though he wanted to. He really did. This need for her made him weak where he'd been strong for far too many years.

"She would if you explained the situation."

"And if someone else found out? If John found out? Right now he can't stop your work; I put you in place, and without a damn good reason, he can't fire you. We have time to build your rep with the board. I won't risk giving him an excuse to use against you."

"Alex—"

Reaching the end of his patience, he gripped her arms carefully and gave her a little shake. "No." He smoothed the spot he'd grabbed, feeling like a bastard as frustrated tears gathered in her eyes. "No, Sara Beth. I will not risk your future. I won't back down now, not when things are finally going right." No matter how crazy it was making him.

His resolve seemed to sink in, and instead of continuing the argument, Sara Beth blinked away her tears, reached up, and rubbed her thumbs softly below his eyes, right where he knew dark circles rested. "You're not sleeping enough."

"Every time I close my eyes, I see her." The words slipped past his guard and out of his mouth before he had a chance in hell of catching them.

"God." Sara Beth breathed the word into the space between them. "Alex—"

He shook his head, jostling her hands. "Don't."

She studied him for a moment, acceptance and frustration warring in her expressive face. Finally a hint of humor sparked, and Sara Beth allowed the moment to pass. "Well, I didn't think I'd ever hear anything that sweet from you. Just what I've always said—it's nice when a man is in touch with his feminine side."

He followed her lead with a grateful sigh. "Nah. It's just the beginning of a midlife crisis. I'm going nuts…quickly. Next thing you know, I'll have a convertible and hair plugs." Just no young thing on his arm, thank you very much.

Sara Beth rubbed the thick thatch of black hair spiking across the top of his head and leaned in close to hug him at the same time. "Somehow," she whispered in his ear, "I don't think Cailin would mind."

Chapter Seven

The door to the cab refused to stay open while she struggled with her overnight bag and clothes and purse and… She bumped the thing hard with her hip, only to have it recoil and hit her back with a force she knew would leave a bruise.

"Need some help?"

Looking over her shoulder, Cailin saw Ian tugging on the door. He leaned against it with a casual grace any man—or woman, for that matter—would envy. "Thanks. Too much stuff to pull out. I still don't understand why I have to go to this dinner tonight."

"Because Alex said so," he teased before grabbing her hanging garment bag from her arms. The dress inside had cost way more than she or her credit card cared to think about, but the charity/business event was formal, and only the upper crust of the upper class here in Atlanta were invited. Sara Beth had given her the name of a designer, and Cailin had found a dress, the least expensive one she actually liked. The fact that her hand shook as she paid for it, she'd tried to ignore.

"Besides," Ian said, "it will be fun: I'll be there."

Cailin rolled her eyes. *The Flirt strikes again.*

"So why are you arriving in a cab?" Ian asked.

"Car trouble." When she'd gone out to leave for work, her engine wouldn't even hint at turning over. She could have asked a neighbor for a jump, assuming it was the battery or starter or alternator or whatever, but today of all days, she had needed to be in the office, and calling a cab was faster than finding a neighbor who was both still home and willing to help. Besides, she'd be out late tonight, and a cab was safer downtown than trying to walk to and from a parking garage.

"Ah. So this"—Ian hefted the bag in his arms—"is what you need to get ready. Personally I think you're overdoing it. You don't need nearly this much stuff to make a beautiful woman even more beautiful."

"I'm already late, Ian," Cailin reminded him, though his bull was flattering to her somewhat depleted ego after her decidedly unfruitful trip to Thrice last weekend and a long week with too much work to do. She was feeling frazzled and forgotten. Ian's easy charm at least helped her smile.

"Well, in you go," he scolded, ushering her into the elevator.

When the doors opened on their floor, Sara Beth just happened to be passing by. Cailin sighed, doing her best to keep it unnoticeable. What was this, a convention?

"Cailin!" The woman took in her and Ian's laden arms. "What's all this?"

Ian's runaway mouth was at least good for some things. Cailin let him explain as she made her way toward the office.

Something about the eerie silence as she rounded the corner near Tammy's desk had the hair on Cailin's nape standing on end. It was after eight thirty; normally by now Tammy's reception area was hopping with people and the constant ringing of the phone and Tammy's happy chatter that ran nonstop all day. Instead even the air was still, motionless. Tense.

What the heck…?

Cailin picked up speed, but when she stepped into the open reception area, Tammy wasn't in sight. Instead the broad shoulders of a big man blocked her from view as he leaned over the desk, his posture threatening.

The faint *hiss* of whispered words reached Cailin's ears as she moved toward the side of the desk. Tammy came into view, her pale face and trembling form cowering back from the aggressive bend of James Allen's body. His venomous tone faded as he straightened, but the angry-bull look he threw her way made clear he wasn't happy at the interruption. His words agreed.

"What do you want?"

She'd dealt with angry men before—what secretary hadn't?—but that didn't stop her gut from clenching or her hands from starting to shake. She tightened her spine and, totally ignoring Allen, said, "Tammy?"

"Cailin." The relief in that sweet Southern twang made Cailin ball up her fists.

"Can we help you, Mr. Allen?" Sara Beth asked.

Cailin turned to Alex's wife, looking past her in puzzlement at Ian's absence. Where had the darn man gone?

Apparently Allen noted the female-only status of his audience as well, because he didn't bother to hide his contempt. "Why would I need you to help me, woman? Unless you've got balls hidden in those nice, tight pants covering your ass— But no." He shook his head, and sarcasm twisted his lips. "If there was,

91

John would've put you in charge, wouldn't he?" He slid a slick tongue across his puffy lips as he leaned sideways to ogle Sara Beth's slender body. "'Sides, I'd definitely be able to see 'em if they were there."

"Sara Be—"

At Tammy's words, Allen's hand snapped out. Whether to backhand the trembling blonde or grab the hand that reached instinctively toward the man threatening her boss, Cailin didn't know. All she knew was the need to protect swirled with a faint—very faint—ribbon of defiance at the man's ugly words. Whatever the reason, her arm automatically shot out, knocking Allen's down and away from Tammy. At the slap of sound when they made contact, every molecule of air in the room disappeared—it was all sucked in at the collective gasp of their frozen little group. Allen's face mottled with rapidly rising, purple fury. And then he lunged toward her.

"Why you little—"

"Allen."

Still stumbling backward, her heart in her throat, Cailin didn't register Alex's voice for a moment. The sudden sagging of her body as relief rushed through her veins took her back a couple more steps until Alex's chest against her shoulder blades stopped her. His muscles were rigid, hard, but his hands were tender, careful as he gathered her to him, steadying her. Did she imagine him lingering against her? Imagine the concern telegraphing itself through Alex's touch on her skin?

Then the moment was gone, and time returned to light speed.

"What the hell is going on here?"

Ian's indelicate snort sounding from behind Alex shouted that the answer to Alex's question was obvious. Ian must have gone down to the office to fetch help.

And his decision proved wise, since with the men's appearance, Allen's entire demeanor changed. Unmistakably caught, he fell back on bluster. "Alex, well, of course... Just a misunderstanding, son, that's all."

Three sets of feminine eyes fastened on the man in clear disbelief. Sara Beth broke their silence. "I don't think so," she said icily. "Maybe I'm not the one who needs to grow some balls."

I think you've got plenty, Cailin thought as Alex stepped away from her and moved toward his wife. Ian's muffled laughter agreed.

"Mind enlightening me?" Alex asked as he clasped Sara Beth's hand in one of his.

A sly smirk curled Sara Beth's taut mouth. "Not really. I think it would be better if Mr. Allen showed himself out. He needs time to think about his actions."

A time-out. Tammy's nervous giggle reflected what all of them were probably thinking. Including Allen, if the rage on his face was anything to go by. With a sharp jerk of his head, he started for the hall. "I'll return this afternoon, Alex."

"Be sure someone from security sends up advance notice first," Alex replied, seeming totally unconcerned as the other man's hands curled into threatening fists before he headed toward the elevators.

None of them moved until the *ding* of the elevator's arrival and the quiet *whoosh* of the doors opening and closing had passed. A collective sigh passed the women's lips, and then Tammy burst into tears, breaking their frozen tableau.

Cailin hurried around the desk and took the woman in her arms. Tammy crumpled, sagging in Cailin's hold. When she looked up, Ian came around and took the woman from her, murmuring quiet words in Tammy's ear as he maneuvered her into her desk chair.

Alex had his arms wrapped around Sara Beth. Cailin tried hard not to watch, not to allow her jealousy to surge, not to even acknowledge that there was a reason to be jealous, but the protective curve of his body drew her gaze like a magnet. Sara Beth's trembling was obvious from where Cailin stood, but from the look on the woman's face and the angry "Rat bastard!" filtering across the room, Cailin didn't think it was fear causing the woman's shaking. Alex ran his hands up and down the length of her spine, soothing her, asking questions, trying to get the whole story. It was mesmerizing and loving and heartbreaking. Sean had never held her like that, never defended her from the world. And before her emotions had thawed, she could have watched and only numbly admired how Alex cared for his wife. But today, it just made her realize all the more how much she wanted him, and the need rising inside her, not just to be held as the other women were being held, but to be held by *Alex*, tore ragged holes in the deepest, most secret parts of her soul.

Wrapping her arms tight around her waist, she stood mute, rocking slightly, desperate to hold the pieces of herself together for just a few minutes longer.

"Cailin."

Jerking her head toward Ian, Cailin raised a brow.

Patting their sobbing secretary on the back, Ian asked, "You okay?"

"Sure. No problem."

A frown crinkled the skin between his concerned gray eyes. "Cail—"

Suddenly Alex's hot, masculine scent surrounded her. "Let me see your wrist," he said.

Her hand plopped into his as if it had a mind of its own. Looking beyond him, she watched warily as Sara Beth looked on, but only worry stared back. No jealousy. No calculated appraisal of Alex's hands on her. Just one woman's concern for another.

Darn it, why did they all have to be so nice? It just made her feel that much more of a slut. The phantom feel of a slithering *S* circled around her heart.

Alex's fingertips rubbed the dark red spot on her wrist. "Seems okay," he said, the low growl in his tone promising retribution.

Slowly Cailin eased her hand back, clearing her throat of any huskiness before she spoke. "It's fine."

"I'm notifying security not to let him in the building without an escort. That man's a menace to women," Sara Beth snapped.

"You ain't kiddin'," Tammy drawled, her voice gravelly from her tears. "Usually there's too many people in here for him to try anything other than a few suggestive remarks, but still..." She lifted red-rimmed eyes to Alex, almost in apology. "He wanted"—a shudder racked her frame—"well, what he wanted was obvious. When I refused, he threatened me." The last words were barely above a whisper.

"Not anymore," Sara Beth promised.

"That's right," Alex said. "From now on, I'll have Barton escorting him to and from my office. You know that security guard has a soft spot for you, honey." He chuckled at Tammy's faint blush. "We'll make sure nothing like this happens again. He may be John's 'old buddy,' but he's not mine." Reaching across the desk, he chucked Tammy's trembling chin. "Okay?"

The secretary released a relieved sigh and nodded. "Okay."

Turning back to Sara Beth and Cailin, he asked, "How did you end up here at just the right time?"

Ian chuckled. "Cosmic convergence."

Sara Beth smiled, the action genuine, bright, then snapped her fingers. "That's right. We've got to get that looked at, Cailin."

"Get what looked at?" Alex asked.

"Cailin's car is on the fritz," Ian answered. "That's why she was late. And a good thing too."

When Alex looked at her, Cailin shrugged. "Must be the battery or something. Ian was helping me bring my stuff upstairs for tonight." Turning, she noticed her purse and case on the ground near the desk. She hadn't even realized she'd dropped it. Presumably Ian had dumped the rest of her stuff when he went to get Alex.

Alex's frown lowered his brows, giving his face a brooding look that was way too sexy. "Look up Jason's. It's on my contact list," he directed Cailin. "They'll go out and take a look."

"No, I—"

"Yes. No arguments. We have work to do, and I'm not sitting around waiting on you to arrive because your car isn't reliable. Like this morning," he pointed out.

"Even though it was a good thing," Ian reiterated.

"This time."

Since she hadn't been late or even had a day off since she'd started the job, Cailin opened her mouth to argue. She wasn't apologizing for something she couldn't help or foresee.

"He's right, Cailin," Sara Beth said. "Let us help you. The owner of the garage is a friend; he'll do a good job, we promise."

Seeing that Sara Beth wanted to smooth things over and knowing she still had a ton of work to do today before their evening appointment at the gala, Cailin reluctantly nodded.

"Good." Alex headed down the hall, leaving Cailin to hastily retrieve her things and hurry after their little trio, throwing an apologetic look over her shoulder at Tammy. In their office, Alex took in the garment bag draped over her desk. He raised his brows in an I'm-not-even-gonna-ask expression and turned back to his inner sanctum. Ian chuckled, gave Sara Beth a quick peck on the cheek, then disappeared. Sara Beth waved at Cailin and followed Alex through his door. Cailin shook her head, sighed, and put everything away. Alex was right; they had work to do.

∞

By the time six o'clock rolled around, Cailin was even more frantic than she'd been on her way to work. She hadn't stopped going all day, including lunch, which had consisted of a can of soda and a granola bar from her desk drawer. In fifteen minutes she was supposed to meet the rest of the group down in the lobby, and she hadn't begun to get ready yet. Fingering the wisps of hair dangling from her hasty twist this morning, she knew she didn't have enough time. It would take her a good five minutes to get to the employee restroom, much less getting all her things out and on.

But... She shook her frazzled head. She couldn't. Any semblance of intimacy was best avoided, and Alex would definitely disapprove.

Not if he doesn't know. It can't hurt if you're the only one who's aware of it, can it?

Glancing once more at the ticking clock, she gathered her things and headed into his office. Alex had a private bath, complete with shower, sink, and all the amenities. She could do more and get ready faster—and didn't have to waste five minutes walking down the hall.

Splaying her makeup and hair accessories across the counter, Cailin hastily stripped out of her clothes and washed down. Lotion dried to a powdery finish across her flushed skin as she completed a hasty makeup job she hoped would hold up to all the expensive makeovers she was certain would be visible tonight. Sometimes being in the background was a good thing, and she had a feeling tonight would be one of those nights. A few strokes with the brush, some hastily placed pins, and her hair fell in just the right mix of updo and seductive tendrils—she hoped.

Her dress's peacock hues glistened on the hanger as she surveyed it critically. She had shoes to match, but the first hurdle was her underwear. The lacy strapless bra cupped her breasts lovingly, the mounds spilling over the top in a display that was wasted on Cailin. The matching thong slid on easily, but it was the garter and stockings that gave her the most trouble. They weren't hard to put on; rather it was the knowledge that the last time she wore them, Alex had been the one to remove them that made her hands shake and struggle with the clasps. The slide of the silk against her skin brought tears to her eyes. She bent, her foot resting atop the closed toilet lid, and focused on straightening the toe, then lacing her peacock-blue shoe over the top of her foot to avoid thinking about the moisture pooling in her eyes—and why it was there.

"Cailin."

Her muscles froze at the dark, seductive voice calling her name. He was close, probably in the doorway. Mortified to be caught in this position, she forced herself to stand, to place her foot on the floor, to take a deep—very deep—breath before turning her head toward Alex.

Whose gaze was riveted on her body.

Did he remember the garter? Did his hands tremble to remove it, just as hers trembled in sweet desperation for him to do so?

She kept her back firmly to him. "Alex! I didn't know—"

Alex licked his lips, gaze sinking down her back to zero in on her mostly bare bottom, and all thought left Cailin's head. She stood, a fierce pride beginning to well in her chest, as the man she cared for more than she should devoured her with a look. Hunger burned bright in his brown irises, firing a similar need in her core, and the tremors moved from her hands to her legs as they clamped hard against a sudden rush of liquid arousal.

Oh God, don't let him see.

"Turn around."

Her eyelids closed involuntarily, the gravelly sound of his voice overwhelming her, but she fought to open them, knowing there was something she needed to do, something just beyond her reach that would save her soul before she damned it for all eternity, before she gave in to her desperate desire for this man and did as he asked.

"Turn around, Cailin," he said again.

Chapter Eight

She shook her head, refusing to look at him.

Alex stepped into the room, the sound of the door clicking shut behind him clanging like a death knell. Cailin turned then and brought her hand up to ward him off. At the sight of her barely covered breasts, however, Alex's control seemed to break into a million tiny shards. He charged, his eyes wild, his big body a two-hundred-pound semi headed straight for her. With heart-stopping speed, he was on her, his hands lifting, carrying, until Cailin found herself against the wall, her back arching away from the tiles' air-conditioned coolness, the force of Alex's chest shackling her in place anyway.

"Ale—"

His tongue was in her mouth before the word was complete. Helpless, completely overtaken, Cailin surrendered. The vague sensations of limbs moving, fabric whispering, all of it was lost in the sheer relief of having his body against her, his mouth fused to hers once more. She'd felt like she would die without him, but here he was, filling her up, consuming her, bringing her to life once more. When his bare chest slammed into hers, she moaned, straining, needing to get closer. She needed to fuse herself to him, be one with him. Know he would never leave her again, not even for—

"Alex, where are you?"

The words rang in some distant part of her brain, but Alex's lips were sliding down her neck, his mouth latching on to the lace-covered, supersensitive tip of her breast, and she was too busy squirming and thrusting her nipple deeper between his lips to pay attention to anything else. Just a little harder, a little faster. Just one more deep suck and she just might explode.

Alex growled, the sound vibrating down her nerve endings and detonating between her legs. Cailin screamed, the pleasure blinding, all-consuming, closing out everything around her—including the *click* of the doorknob as it turned.

"Alex, are you… Oh!"

When his mouth left her breasts, Cailin grabbed his head, trying to bring it back, needing to prolong the ripples of pleasure traveling through her body. She needed—

"Cailin!" The harsh word acted like a slap in the face. She surfaced, startled, and stared into Alex's angry brown eyes. What had she done wrong? Another spasm jerked through her, and what seemed to be disgust twisted the corner of his mouth. Cailin turned her head, desperate to avoid the look that was seared into her eyeballs.

And met Sara Beth's confused gaze.

Oh…God. Oh no. No. She hadn't. She wouldn't… But she had. A devastated sob burst from her; she tried to catch it with her palm, slapping it over her mouth to control the sound, but too late. It lingered there between the three of them, evidence of her guilt. Her humiliation. Her sick need for a man who didn't belong to her. Closing her eyes against Sara Beth's pain protected no one, but Cailin did it instinctively, like a child covering their eyes so an adult couldn't find them. Her mind knew Sara Beth still stood in the doorway, gaze taking in her husband holding another woman—a mostly naked woman—but logic fled, and all she could do was hide, even if only behind her tight, wet eyelids.

"Cailin, shhh, it's all—"

No, she couldn't take that from him. She had to get away, get out of this room, get covered. She began to fight him, clawing like a wildcat, twisting, desperate to escape, to lick her wounds in private.

"Alex." Sara Beth's voice.

Cailin felt his head turn. "Out," he yelled. The sound froze Cailin into stillness, as if the lack of movement could hide her as well as her closed eyelids had. Alex never yelled at Sara Beth. She was too sweet, too delicate. She didn't deserve to be yelled at, not like Cailin.

"But—"

"Please." The word was milder, entreating. "I'll join you in a moment."

Silence. Then the door clicked closed. Alex sighed, his breath gusting across the exposed skin of her shoulder, the upper crest of her breast. The betrayal of her nipple puckering in response nauseated her. How could she? How could she?

Alex stepped back, his hands releasing her, his support gone. Cailin let herself fold down, arms wrapped around her knees, her forehead coming slowly to rest on top as she tried to meld her back with the cold tile wall behind her. There was nowhere to run, to hide. All she could do was cover her body and pray he left before her mind totally shattered.

Minutes later a warm, fuzzy white towel settled around her back. Alex's hand skimmed her wet, swollen cheek. She jerked back. She deserved this. She'd lusted after a man she'd known was married, had allowed him to touch her after she'd known he was married. She deserved whatever she got. She just prayed, for Sara Beth's sake, that what she'd done had not destroyed the other woman's obvious love for Alex completely.

"Cailin." When she didn't raise her head, Alex forced her chin up with uncompromising fingers. He stared deeply into her eyes, unreadable, unblinking. After several minutes he said, "Come into the office after you clean up."

She shook her head. She couldn't; she wanted escape.

"Yes, you will. Don't worry about the gala; I'll take care of it. Now clean up and come to me."

The slow, simmering burn of resentment rose in her belly, but Cailin nodded. If it would grant her a few minutes alone to gather the shards of her heart and pride, she would agree. Nothing else could carry her through the humiliation waiting on the other side of that door.

Alex gave her chin a hard shake. "Answer me."

"Okay," she snapped as she jerked her chin out of his hold, narrowly avoiding banging her head into the wall. Looking at him again—no, she couldn't do it. She just needed a few minutes. Then she'd face the music like a good girl. She'd never known how to be anything else until she'd divorced Sean. Until she'd met Alex.

His satisfaction worked its way under her skin even though she couldn't see it in his eyes. The hand hovering near her face dropped to her arm, gave a slight squeeze, and he was out the door, the sound of it closing the most comforting thing she thought she'd ever heard.

Taking another deep breath, Cailin steadied herself, stood, and started to dress.

ALEX STARED AT his shaking hand as he closed the door to the bathroom. Instinctively his grip tightened on the doorknob, his only connection to the woman on the other side. Cailin had stolen his control faster than he'd ever dreamed possible.

"God, Alex, I am so, so sorry."

Rubbing his other hand roughly down his face, then back up to partially cover his eyes, he turned to Sara Beth. Words couldn't express the jumble taking over his head right now, nor did he want them to. All he could do was shake his head back and forth, hoping his complete lack of...anything...communicated its way to her.

Sara Beth seemed to get it. Of course, she usually did. Walking over, she grabbed his still-quivering biceps and firmly dragged him away from the door. Once they reached the opposite wall, where their conversation wouldn't filter through the door and upset Cailin further, she hugged him. "I couldn't find you. Ian went ahead to the dinner, and I told him we'd follow as soon as you came back. But you didn't." Now it was her turn to shake her head. "I would never have done that to Cailin." She peeked up at him, arms still wrapped around his churning gut and the lifeless limbs dangling at his sides. "You, maybe, but not Cailin."

Alex didn't laugh. He couldn't even smile. His mind remained across the room, in that bathroom with Cailin.

"Alex." A rough shake caught his attention. "Get a grip. She's gonna be out here any minute. You've got to tell her."

Again with the head shaking. Where had all his smooth words fled to?

Sara Beth donned that stubborn face he knew from vast experience didn't bode well for whatever he decreed. "Look," she growled, "either you tell her, or I will."

"Tell me what?" a wobbly voice asked behind him.

"Cailin." Alex turned to face her. The sight of her, pale and stricken, tackled him to the ground and practically wrestled him into submission. The need to make it all better rose with every thump of his heart. He strode across the room, hands outstretched, but the minute he stepped into her space, she jerked away. Venom flashed in her eyes. She turned not to him but to Sara Beth, who looked on with compassion.

Cailin's words came out as stiff as her spine. "Please don't touch me."

It was the "please" that gnawed his heart in two like a dull knife. Raising his stare to the ceiling, he clenched his teeth and tried to breathe. Helplessness was not in his skill set. There had to be some way to fix this.

Sara Beth stepped toward them. "Cailin—"

The woman next to him tensed even further, brittle enough to break, and he had to reach out to touch her. He couldn't help it. That imperative, protective part of his brain refused to let her suffer this alone. His brain zeroed in on the thought, focusing, and he felt the rightness centering him deep inside. The chaos fell away; determination settled in its place. The decision was made, for good or bad. Either way, he was about to find out if the truth would damn him.

He encircled her wrist, ignoring her instinctive jerk away. "You're right, Sara Beth. We have to explain. It's not fair to do anything else." He gestured toward the sofa arrangement at one end of the office suite. "Come sit down, sweetheart."

Refusal immediately blanketed her face.

"Sit down, Cailin." He could practically see several choice words gathering behind her lips. Hoping to forestall them, he added, "Please. We won't hurt you." *At least, not any more than I already have.*

"God, no. Please, Cailin," Sara Beth pleaded.

A reluctant nod. A careful step, as if the ground would fall out from beneath her at any moment—or already had. Cailin made her way toward the love seat and settled herself in the middle, leaving no room for someone to sit with her. Alex discounted the obvious message and sat on the coffee table facing her, his knees caging hers, eliminating the possibility of escape. Sara Beth took the end position on the couch, kitty-corner to them.

"Caili—"

Sara Beth stopped as Cailin bent at the waist, her face coming to rest on her knees, and burst into tears. Alex reached out, hands hovering, uncertain what to do. Sara Beth shook her head. They both leaned forward, their heads coming together close to Cailin's. Her words were mostly lost in the sobs, but Alex understood enough to guess it had all become too much for her. If she'd been as stressed as he had this last month, the situation tearing at her as it had at him, then the pain and humiliation of being walked in on—the cryfest made perfect sense. He almost wished he could join her.

"I tried... And Sara B-B-Beth... And I had... And you... I'm an ad-dulter-ress-s." She choked. "I-I never..."

Alex held out trembling hands as she rocked forward, then back, seriously wondering if he would have to catch her at any minute. A desperate glance in Sara Beth's direction showed the other woman in tears as well.

God Almighty, get me out of here. He had to do something, or he was going to lose it.

Grabbing Cailin's arms, he shook her gently. "Cailin! Get it together. You're not—" No, that would take a bit more explaining. "It's all right. Stop, sweetheart. Listen to me."

If his words registered, there was no sign of it. They registered with Sara Beth, though, because she glared at him and slapped his hands away. He sat back, hiding his sigh of gratitude that someone knew what to do. He certainly didn't.

Ignoring the fact that there wasn't enough room for her, Sara Beth shoved her pixie-sized body into the tiny gap on the love seat and forced Cailin into her arms. She rocked the other woman, murmuring soothing sounds. Alex waited. As the sobbing lessened and Cailin calmed, so did he. Witnessing her pain, he called himself ten kinds of asshole. How in hell would he ever repair what he'd allowed to become so irreparably broken?

When only the sound of ragged breathing filled the air between them, Sara Beth finally spoke, her tone brooking no argument.

"Cailin, I want you to listen to me. It's all right. You didn't do anything wrong."

Cailin raised a heavy head. "But—"

"I'm a lesbian."

Cailin's double take would have been comical if not for the tear tracks ruining the usually pink-and-cream perfection of her cheeks. "You're a what?"

Now it was Sara Beth's turn to stiffen. Alex knew she hadn't shared this information with more than a couple of people, himself included. The sensitivity was expected.

"Sara Beth isn't in love with me," Alex explained. "She likes women, not men."

"But…so…" Cailin's caramel-colored eyes brimmed with confusion. "Why…?"

"My father," Sara Beth said, apparently following Cailin's stuttered train of thought better than Alex. "He's very…traditional. I've been groomed since I was a teen to have some role in the company, but Dad refuses to allow anyone of the female gender"— her fingers crooked into air quotes—"to lead his precious empire."

"Without a marriage, Sara Beth stood no chance of inheriting as she deserves. In fact, John threatened to leave a hundred percent of his money, not just his company, to someone else if she didn't have a ring on her finger by the time she turned thirty-five."

Cailin seemed to find her tongue. "Why not just let him?"

Sara Beth shrugged. "I could, and if it were just the money, I would. But not the company. Too many people depend on my family, on *me* to support them, to take care of their families. I can't allow that responsibility to go to just anyone after my father retires. I need to take care of them myself." A tiny smirk tilted the edge of her mouth. "And because I'm too damn stubborn to accept the word 'no.' I've pushed myself to be the best, to earn the right to run the company I love. I won't let the fact that I have the wrong private parts stop me from fulfilling that dream. But Dad refused to give me a chance. He wanted a man to run the company. He wanted a ring on my finger, so we gave him one, sort of."

Cailin looked at Alex. "So you..."

Alex allowed his fingers to finally tangle in the blonde snarls outlining her face. "I volunteered." No way in hell would he have let Sara Beth do this alone, or risk her future on some other man.

Cailin jerked backward, away from his touch. The distracted look on her face told him it was mostly reflex, probably left over from the past month, but it burned all the same. She chose that moment to look up, to focus on him. Lord knew what she read in his eyes, but she reached out and took his hand in hers, settling them both on her knee.

"So, you're not...together." Raised eyebrows made clear what Cailin meant.

Sara Beth's pert nose wrinkled. "Ew! No. That would be like going to bed with my brother."

"But it's obvious you love each other."

"We do," Alex assured her. "We've been best friends since we met as teenagers. But we aren't in love." He squeezed her hand hard. "There's no fire. Not anything like it is with *us*."

A pretty pink blush stained her cheeks, a more natural hue than the hot flush her crying jag had left behind.

"Besides," Sara Beth interjected, "Sam wouldn't share."

"Sam?" Cailin blinked. "Oh. Sam."

Sara Beth took her turn blushing. "It's easier to have my 'female friend' sleep over than it is for Alex to have an overnight guest."

"Which is why I haven't. Ever," Alex assured Cailin. "Even while we were engaged. But that night at Thrice, when I saw you…" The impossibility of putting the feeling into words drove him to silence. Cailin nodded, either because she understood or because she'd felt the same way.

Sara Beth punched him lightly in the arm. "Not for lack of trying. I'm not a selfish bitch."

"No, you're a woman who stands to lose everything if her father caught even a hint of scandal," Alex reminded her.

Sara Beth's mouth tightened. "You can't go on like this forever, Alex. As much as I love you, it's not fair for you to be alone."

Cailin added her other hand to the pile on her knee. "He's not."

Her words sparked something in his chest he couldn't identify. Ignoring it, he frowned at her. "You don't know what you're agreeing to. Living in secrecy wears on you. It doesn't get easier; it just gets harder."

Cailin opened her mouth to speak, paused, glanced at Sara Beth, then seemed to come to a decision. "Alex, I want you. I…care about you."

Shock kept him silent for a long moment. "You what?"

She firmed her shoulders. "I care, Alex. This month has been…"

"Hell."

"Yes."

Fire shot through his veins. Alex leaned forward and took her face between his hands. The kiss was hot and carnal and everything he really wanted it to be. It didn't end until Sara Beth cleared her throat, then finally gave a loud, laughing, "Hey!" to break them apart. Being able to see Cailin's bemused smile made the interruption worth it.

"I want you too, Cailin." Alex spoke from his heart, and his voice cracked with emotion by the end of those five little words.

"And that sounds like my cue to get outta here," Sara Beth teased. She stood and looked down at them both. Then she brushed Alex's cheek with a sweet kiss. "Congrats, Alex."

Questions remained—a lot of them—but for tonight, he let them go. Instead he smiled. "Thanks."

Cailin stood from the love seat. She stepped tentatively toward Sara Beth, then enveloped the other woman in a fervent hug, turned her face into Sara Beth's neck, and whispered fiercely, "Thank you. Your secret is safe with me."

Sara Beth gripped her tight and whispered something Alex couldn't hear in her ear. Cailin stepped back with a laugh and brushed stray tears from her cheeks.

Sara Beth headed for the door. "Don't worry about tonight. Ian has enough presence for all of us put together. Take the night off."

As if he'd planned on anything else. Alex raised a brow at Cailin. "You heard the lady. Go get your stuff. We're going home."

"We are?"

"Absolutely." He leaned close, her scent surrounding him, and breathed against her ear, "I've waited a long time to have you again. You've got five minutes. Then you're mine."

Chapter Nine

For some reason, Cailin had expected Alex to jump her the minute the door closed on her tiny house. The frantic groping in the bathroom had shown evidence of desperate need, a need she more than shared. But Alex seemed to have other ideas.

Leaning back against the closed door, he drank her in. Cailin dropped her bags, for once not anxious or nervous or afraid. Instead she waited, confident that the man standing in front of her wanted her, needed her with an aching urgency that matched her own. Even if she hadn't been, the words that escaped his mouth would have convinced her.

"God, sweetheart. I just keep waiting to wake up and find out this is a dream."

It wasn't an admission of love—she wasn't even sure she wanted one. Their situation was too complex, too rife with the possibility for heartache. But they were exactly what she needed to hear.

Tears gathered, but she shook them away. This was no time for tears. That time had passed. Now was the time for her and Alex. Holding her arms out from her sides, she said, "I'm right here. Touch me if you don't believe it."

Molten heat flashed across his face. He tensed, lifting his body away from the door, and began a slow stalk across the room. Cailin backed away on weak legs, stumbling blindly down the hall, dragging her hands along the walls to help guide her in the dark. But Alex she saw clearly. Fire blazed in his eyes, so hot she felt beads of sweat gathering between her breasts.

"The shirt." His voice rumbled, vibrating along her spine. The buttons resisted her trembling efforts and concentrating as she walked backward didn't help, but finally her shirt slid down her arms, leaving mostly bare skin to Alex's sight. He purred his pleasure, then commanded, "Bra."

The smile she struggled to hold back stretched her mouth wide. She couldn't contain it, couldn't contain the joy bursting inside. She reached behind her back, undid the clasp, and slowly shrugged her bra off, allowing the cool air access to her overwarm skin. She bumped into the hall wall.

Alex grinned too, but his smile was all teeth. "Skirt."

One step. Two. The button gave, then the zipper. The stretchy material clung to her legs, hindering her next step, the little shimmy she gave to free it setting her breasts jiggling in a way that caused Alex to stumble. Femininity and freedom filled her as the cloth finally slid the rest of the way to her feet. Oh yes, she liked this.

The doorway to her bedroom loomed behind her. Cailin caught one edge, using it for leverage as she lifted a leg to unhook the blue shoes she still wore. Alex growled and shook his head. "Uh-uh."

Tilting her head at his gruff command, she allowed her hand to meander its way back up her leg, drawing attention to hills, caressing valleys, beckoning the man who watched to trace the same path all the way to the vee of her thighs. Bold as brass, she stroked the strip of lace that made up the thong she wore. Moisture wet the delicate fabric.

"Touch it," Alex said.

A single digit responded to his command. She dipped her chin to look down and sent her finger swirling in slow, titillating circles around the swollen nub of her clit, barely brushing the sensitive tip, sending her desire soaring. The act's effect on Alex was equally explosive. He hurtled down the hallway, tackling her as he reached the doorway and carrying her across the room to land on the bed in five seconds flat. Cailin laughed as she flopped onto her back. Alex's momentum carried him right over her; his grip on her hips pulled her into a sitting position on top of his firm lower belly.

Cailin rested her forearms on Alex's chest, leaned down to bring them together, and kissed him. Firm lips met soft, and both parted, tongues dueling in a drugging tussle where neither needed to win. The contact was enough. Cailin put all she could into the touch, conveying her need with every thrust, her lingering pain with every nip, and, overriding it all, the elation her skin simply couldn't contain.

"Alex." The word hitched against his lips.

"Cailin," he teased. A soft smile pulled his mouth away from hers. "Sit up."

"You are overdressed," she pointed out as she lifted her torso. Dragging her hands down his body sent a thrill up her arms as the heavy beat of his heart and the quickening of his breath were revealed. And beneath her, the heavy push of his erection nudged her backside. She wanted that solid shaft inside her, filling her up. She needed it. Now.

"So do something about it."

Lifting up to her knees, she went to scoot backward. Alex's hands gripped her arms.

"Oh no you don't."

"But—"

A long, rough finger settled against her lips. "Improvise."

Rolling her eyes, she grabbed the waistband of his dress pants. A sharp *pop* startled her before heat flashed through her butt. "Alex! You spanked me, you…" The rest trailed off as that heat settled between her legs and cream responded in abundance.

"And there's more where that came from," he assured her as he rubbed the hot spot he'd smacked. "Now get a move on—without the sass." His grin was downright wicked.

So that was the way he wanted to play it, huh? Ignoring his clothes for a moment, Cailin reached behind her, allowing the escaping tendrils of her hair to slowly filter through her fingers. One by one, she dug out the pins holding the heavy pile in place. Alex stared, his thumbs rubbing absently along her inner thighs as her mass of curls did a leisurely slide down to her shoulders. Tendrils settled over the tops of her breasts. When she tipped her head forward, long bangs hid what she was sure was a sneaky smile. Alex growled, the sound rising to a soft whine as she leaned down and took the tab of his zipper in her teeth. His shaft jumped, bumping her chin as she carefully, deliberately opened his pants.

"Cailin," he moaned.

Fragrant heat hit her nose as the placket parted. Dipping farther, she nuzzled his shaft, his tangy, masculine scent overpowering her senses like a drug. Her core clenched. On instinct, she grabbed the tails of his dress shirt and pulled. Buttons pinged across the room. Alex arched, his fingers digging deep into her thighs. "God, yes!"

Satisfaction settled like fizz in her chest. It must have bubbled up to her expression as well, because when Alex's gaze focused once more, he quirked a dark brow at her. "Happy?"

She feasted on the sight of his muscled chest, the trail of dark hair marching from his navel to the heavy thatch surrounding his sex, and her mouth watered. "Absolutely."

Alex slid his hands up to grip her hips and lifted her. "Good. Hold me," he directed. Cailin grasped his firm length in her hand, lingering, beginning a soft pump before Alex lowered her onto him. He dropped her, letting gravity pull her down until the head of his erection hit the end of her channel, and Cailin felt truly taken, deep down to her soul.

Head thrown back, all she could do was clench around him. Her body stretched and pulsed, unwillingly accommodating, enveloping him in a way that made them both groan.

When she would have started a slow ride, Alex forced her to stillness. "No. It's my turn."

Refusing to let her move, Alex took his time, his hands playing across her skin until she was certain she would go insane. The need to move, to rub her aching clit against him and bring herself to orgasm, rode her hard, but Alex was having none of it. He traced her veins, seeming enthralled with the blue lines underneath her skin. When those veins intersected at her nipples, he sampled the textures along her areolae. A delicate pinch to one nipple caused a spasm in her pelvis, and they both gasped at the sensation.

Then the game got serious. For every zing of sensation from Alex's touch, Cailin would clench around him. The back-and-forth became a race to see which of them would give in and fall over the edge first. Cailin managed to hold a steady lead until Alex lowered a thumb to his mouth, wet it, and zeroed in on her clit. The sensitive nub was hard and pulsing, the slow circling of his finger creating a ring of fire that burned everything else away until all Cailin could feel was the need to explode. The tightening of her body around his must have had a similar effect on Alex, because soon he was thrusting, pounding up into her, hitting her clit with every stroke, until both of them detonated, obliterating everything but the surge of pleasure in their veins that linked them until they became one.

∞

It took a shower and another round of loving before either he or Cailin could relax, as if their bodies were driven by a hunger only the other's touch could truly satisfy. Even then, Cailin lay in his arms, her pulse quiet but fingers unsteady as they trailed through the hair sprinkled across his chest. Could she feel the thump of his heartbeat, the fear that had his chest aching and his breath shallow long after his climax had receded? He tried hard to hide it, to hide the emotion surging under his skin like a tidal wave, an emotion he wouldn't, couldn't acknowledge without sentencing her to what could be years of pain and frustration.

Stroking the bare, supple skin of her ass, he burrowed his nose into the crook of her neck and shoulder. The words welling up escaped in a soft whisper against her throat. "You deserve so much better than me."

Her heartbeat thumped against him. "No, I deserve you. No matter where this takes us, what happens in the future"—she palmed one firm pec, his nipple pebbling at her touch—"you're a gift, Alex. My gift."

And if he allowed things to progress any further, allowed his need for her to become any stronger, he might become her curse. They hadn't given their relationship or their emotions a name. What would happen when they couldn't avoid it any longer? He shook his head. "I can't give you all of me, not as things stand. That's not fair to you."

Cailin slid her arms around his shoulders, hugging him to her. "Would you have done it differently? If you could have looked into the future and seen me, or someone like me, and known the day would come that you would...need someone this way, would you have refused to help Sara Beth?"

Turning his head, he settled against one mounded breast, drawing on her warmth. Would he have refused? No, absolutely not. Sara Beth was his to care for—she was his best friend, the only real family he still had. Marrying her had been the only solution to their immediate problem, getting Sara Beth into a position where she could prove herself, something they could never have accomplished without Alex's promotion after their engagement. John had owned their lives then, still did to a certain extent. But as much as Alex knew he'd done the right thing, he couldn't shake the feeling that Cailin was his to care for as well, and sometime in the very near future, he would end up failing her. Big-time.

He wanted all of her; instead he had to take what he could get.

"No, I couldn't have changed it," he admitted finally. "She needed me. I made the decision."

Cailin pulled back, caramel eyes shining. "Exactly. That's what makes you the man you are, Alex. You would give anything for someone you love, and not just because of what they give back to you." She rubbed a finger along his scrunched eyebrow. "I've known from the beginning that you are a strong, honorable man. That's what confused me. My heart knew before my brain and my eyes could catch up."

"Maybe." Wrapping a hand around the back of her neck, he drew her in and took her mouth, delving deep, and in that moment he wished to the depths of his soul that he was free, damn the consequences. He tucked her head into his shoulder, not wanting her to see his face, the evidence of his struggle, but couldn't help saying, "I would give anything for you. Anything. That's what makes this so hard. Because there will come a point where the burden will become too much, where the secrecy we have to maintain will hurt you. I don't want to hurt you."

"I know." Her lips, then her tongue brushed his neck. "I know."

Chapter Ten

Cailin rubbed her forehead. The ache that had settled there after lunch was not going away. Excedrin, caffeine—none of it had worked. The simple truth was, work was getting to her. With the consortium six weeks away and Keane Industries' research in the final stages of preparation to be presented, they were all working long hours. Her time at work limited her time with Alex, at least her free time with him, the time where they could just be open and together and without the pretenses that filled their day-job lives. She needed that time to stay balanced. Understanding. Resentment-free. Without it, she battled all those negative gremlins determined to whittle away whatever happiness they could find.

"Cailin, can you come in, please?" Alex's voice over the intercom sounded almost as tired as she felt, which just made her feel worse. She was selfish. *S for selfish.* She had an awful lot of *S*'s. As she gathered her netbook and hurried toward the inner office, a stern talking-to resounded in her head to the rhythm of her headache's pounding.

She smiled at Alex as she walked in, settling into the chair in front of his desk while he walked over to grab a bottle of water out of the hidden fridge near the seating area. Opening her netbook, Cailin worked on pulling up a new file while she waited. The silence didn't bother her; she and Alex had settled into a routine here at the office, and she found his lack of talking soothed her—especially when her head felt like it would split open any minute.

The new file opened with a faint *beep*. As Cailin looked down at the screen, a sheaf of papers was shoved between her eyes and the waiting file. "What—"

Alex nuzzled her earlobe. "Surprise."

Cailin took the papers and shuffled through them before she finally absorbed what she was seeing. "Airline tickets?"

Alex's nose bumped her neck when he nodded. "Yep. You, me, and American Airlines."

"But...why?" Was there a meeting she'd missed hearing about?

"Just because." He moved around in front of her. "We need a little break. And trust me, in about two weeks when the research deadline gets down to the wire, that will be impossible. Better take advantage of it while we can."

"Are you sure it's okay?"

"For us to go?"

"For us both to go. Won't someone...?"

"The tickets are for Friday afternoon, coming back in on Sunday night. I'll let everyone know I've given you the afternoon off since I'm gonna be unavailable. What we do outside this office is nobody's business but ours."

Though that wasn't technically true, she decided not to argue; she wanted this too much. "Okay."

Alex looked very much like he wanted to violate their no-kissing-at-work rule, but he didn't. His smile, though, stretched so wide his rarely revealed dimple showed on the left side. "Good. I've got reservations at the Hermitage Hotel in Nashville. Downtown. Five-star. We can have the weekend to relax, just the two of us." He reached up and massaged her temples, a flicker of worry surfacing. "You've been working too hard."

She scoffed. "I'm not the only one."

"I know," he said. "Thanks for letting me give you this."

Leaning slightly closer until his face took over her field of vision, Cailin whispered, "Me, or you?" She tilted her head to the side and gave him a suggestive look, and she saw the moment Alex got her point. Heat surfaced.

"Both," he assured her. "But I'll definitely make it worth your while."

∞

She just bet he would. She held on to those words like a lifeline for the next two days. Thursday night she made a special trip to the mall to shop for lingerie. For the first time ever, she anticipated going away with the man she loved. She hadn't even anticipated her honeymoon—too much anxiety had surrounded her wedding and getting everything just right, jockeying for position against all the other June brides in a town where everyone knew everyone and every event became a competition. By the time the wedding was over, all she'd wanted was to sleep, not have sex, especially not sex that hadn't really been about her pleasure—or even sharing pleasure—at all.

Friday morning she finished packing, then went in to work. Alex sent her home at noon, but he arrived for their trip to the airport an hour after she did. They were in Nashville by dinnertime.

Once they were safely ensconced in their room at the famous Hermitage Hotel, Alex ordered room service. While they waited, he feasted, literally. In a moment strangely reminiscent of their first night together, he seated Cailin on the edge of their massive king-size bed, mounded pillows behind her, then knelt on the carpeted floor, his face between her splayed thighs. The scent of her arousal hit her nose the minute she spread her legs, the tang an obvious aphrodisiac to Alex. He drew the lips of her sex apart, and without preamble, without even so much as a word passing his lips, he latched on to her clit and sucked her in hard. Cailin's orgasm rose within seconds, her body shaking and surging, needing him closer, needing just that one tiny touch to drive her over the edge. Her empty channel pulsed. As if sensing the missing piece so essential to her satisfaction, Alex slid two fingers in, turning them to hook into her G-spot. Cailin went off like a rocket.

The next thing she knew, Alex's mouth was gone, and he was pulling her closer until her bottom hung just over the edge of the bed. "What…?"

Alex shushed her, going right on with arranging her body to his complete satisfaction. Hooking her knees in the crooks of his elbows, he lifted slightly, aligning their bodies. When he bent forward, his thick cockhead met her wet slit. Cailin cried out as he surged deep inside.

The angle was just…God, just unbelievable. The firm sac hanging between his legs slapped just below her opening with every thrust, the crisp hair scraping the sensitive area over and over. But it was inside, where the hard push of his cock scraped her still-clenching walls, that made her eyes roll back in her head. Alex pounded her, his hunger palpable with every move, in every breath. His face tensed, and

Cailin stared, fascinated, as the drive to completion played out for her to see mere inches from her eyes. Then the arm holding one of her knees bent, hard fingers grasped her hand, and Alex brought her fingers down to touch her clit.

Cailin startled. She'd never touched herself with a man staring into her eyes, and a rush of heat hit her veins quicker than anything she'd ever known.

Evidently Alex felt it too. "Fast, sweetheart," he urged, his voice strained. "I won't last long."

Her hips tilted instinctively at the husky sound of his voice, firming the contact with her fingers. She wanted more. Hesitantly she explored their connection, feeling the wet evidence of her desire, the thin skin of lips stretched tight to accommodate him, the heavy weight of his shaft as he surged in and out without hesitation. At her touch, his breath hitched, his eyes glazed over, and he ground into her, hitting the opening to her womb and sparking a flame that flashed out of control. Her fingers flew, building the sensation in her clit as her gaze locked with Alex's, and she savored the craving that built there in his eyes. And finally, strung tight on the wire of need, Cailin hit the pinnacle of sensation and flew back into the abyss. Only the hot surge of Alex's release registered; everything else floated in the ether, unimportant, unwanted...

Until a discreet knock sounded at their door. "Room service, sir."

Regret twinged as Alex kissed her quickly, then backed away, heading to the bath to retrieve one of the fluffy robes hanging there. While he walked through into the suite's living area, Cailin tried to convince herself to move, but right now she resembled nothing so closely as a limp dishrag, so she stayed. When he returned, she still lay half on, half off the bed, just as he'd left her.

Alex chuckled. "Come on, sleepyhead. Dinner's waiting." He urged her up, into the bathroom, where he cleaned and enfolded her in the other fluffy robe while she resented his seemingly clear head. He tugged her into the front room still grumbling.

"Steaks," he said, then chuckled when, aggravation forgotten, she flung herself across the room to lift the lids on the waiting food. The heavenly aroma of grilled meat filled the air, and her mouth watered. She'd told Alex once that she loved a thick, juicy steak better than any other meal, especially when a loaded baked potato shared the plate. He'd obviously remembered.

Annoyance faded, soothed by the fragrant offering. "Thank you."

Alex shrugged. "I got dinner to please you. Dessert is for me."

"Oh really? What did you get?"

"That's for me to know and you to find out."

She grinned. A challenge, huh? She liked this side of Alex. The heavy air that had surrounded him in the club the first night they'd met, the desperation in his eyes, had faded to a hard resolve over the few weeks that followed. If convincing himself to stay away from her took as much willpower for him as it had for her, that didn't surprise her. Now that willpower had been turned into a determination to make their relationship—what little they could have—work. But he never lost that edge, that driven quality unless they were in bed, and sometimes not even then, she thought with a blush, remembering his handling of her not twenty minutes ago. This carefree aspect to his personality was new. He seemed happy. And she was happy to see him happy, silly as it sounded.

The chocolate mousse, they found, contrasted perfectly with her skin and complemented its salty bite, or so Alex said. All she knew was that concentrating on the nuances of flavor exploding on her tongue—and around Alex's cock—went beyond her ability when he also had his tongue on her. Before long they were both hot, sweaty, sticky, and very satisfied. Cailin watched in dazed fascination as a tiny drop of moisture curved around Alex's hip as he knelt above her, trying to catch his breath.

Good luck, she thought, lungs laboring. They might end up going back to work more exhausted, if happier, than when they'd left, if they kept this up. But after another shower and a short argument over whether or not she would wear pajamas—*what if there's a fire?*—they lay spooned together under the covers, bare skin to bare skin. Of course.

THE FEEL OF her against him was like the softest silk. If he hadn't already come twice in the past two hours, he'd have her under him in a heartbeat. As it was, he couldn't convince his dick to subside, so he just cuddled the semihard length against Cailin's full, beautiful ass and wallowed in the pleasure of having her in his arms. No saying good night, no sneaking around—they could pretend for just a little while that this was their life, that none of the rest of it existed, that they could truly and openly be together. That real life existed outside of these three short days, he knew, but for now the ostrich strategy sounded pretty good.

Especially if it meant waking up with Cailin in the morning.

She reached down, and soft fingers brushed the curve of his hip and leg, tangling in the hair covering his thigh. Cailin seemed to like his body hair; she'd spent hours one night just running her hand across his chest. Or maybe it was just the freedom of touching another person and knowing she wouldn't be rebuffed. She'd told him about Sean. The bastard hadn't known what a treasure he possessed. And though Alex hated the pain her ex-husband—hell, everybody in her hometown—had put her through, he couldn't help being damn glad it had brought her to him. Nothing in his life, including his friendship with Sara Beth, had ever made him believe in miracles, not until he held her in his arms.

"How did you and Sara Beth meet?" Cailin asked.

"Funny story." He tilted her back against him, sneaked a hand under the soft mound of her breast, then laid her forward again so that it fell directly into his hand. Experimentally he brought his fingers together, searching for her nipple. The tight tip was in direct alignment. *Perfect.*

He started a steady massage of her breast and listened to her breath quicken as he talked. "Sara Beth is a typical overachiever, but with a father like hers, that's not surprising. In high school she was into everything: beta club, chess, student-body president, debate—you name it, she did it. Except sports."

A slow roll of her nipple. A thumb circling her taut nub.

Cailin cleared her throat. "And?"

129

"And…she also just happened to make prom queen her sophomore year, seriously ticking off the wannabe runner-up, whose boyfriend happened to make prom king."

"Uh-oh."

"Yep." Alex forced his mind to stay on his story and not the slow undulations that had begun in Cailin's hips. "The girl—Roxie was her name…stupid eighties fads—anyway, she decided to make it her mission for Sara Beth to be miserable. The girl harassed her no end, which was fine with Sara Beth. She had no problem fighting with words. It was when the girl got physical that she had a problem. Her and some friends cornered Sara Beth in the locker room one day. Broke her nose."

Cailin cringed. "What did she do?"

"She found me." Alex grinned against her shoulder and moved his hand to her top breast, beginning the same torture there. Cupped in his palm, her breasts felt like firm fruit, ripe for the plucking. "I was on the high school wrestling team."

"You?"

He didn't know if he should be amused or insulted. "Yes, me. Jeez." He pinched her straining nipple. The laugh that escaped him felt almost as good as her body. Almost—nothing could feel *as* good. "Sara Beth is just like her father that way—she always knows where to get the information she needs. So she searched out the captain of the wrestling team, me, and paid me to teach her to fight."

"And did you?"

"Of course I did. Only I wouldn't let her pay me, not with money. She became this poor jock's English tutor. We were stuck together, and the rest... Well, you know what they say."

Cailin nodded.

He couldn't stop touching her. The soft flat of her belly called to him, and he began long, slow strokes from pelvis to shoulder, spreading his fingers wide to cover as much territory as possible in between.

"So..." She hesitated, but he wasn't sure if it was due to uncertainty or his touch. Over her shoulder, he saw the tip of her pink tongue dip out to moisten her lips. Aha. Uncertainty.

"Ask, Cailin. I don't want there to be secrets between us."

Tilting her head to the side, Cailin rubbed against his stubbly cheek, strands of her blonde curls getting caught in the scruff. If she'd been a cat, she would have purred; he was certain of it. He stroked her as if she was, moving all the way down over her hip before smoothing his way back up again.

"So, what did you and Cailin plan for this...marriage? Will it just keep going? Will her father ever...?" Cailin clamped her lips shut. She'd never broached this subject with him, and now that she had, he found himself both wary and elated. Elated because it meant she felt she had enough of a stake in him to risk it, and wary because, well...

"Honestly, at first we didn't have a plan. John was putting so much pressure on Sara Beth, and at the time no one knew about her sexual orientation, not even me."

"She didn't tell you?"

"I guessed, but I didn't talk to her about it. I figured if she wanted me to know, she'd get around to it. But she never did. It probably would have gone on like that for years if I hadn't put my foot down." He traced a circle around the indentation of her belly button. "She got sick. Mono. She wasn't taking care of herself, and I could tell she had become severely depressed. I didn't—and still don't—give a fuck whether she likes men or women. I wanted her healthy."

"And so you made sure she got healthy."

"Yeah." Cailin knew him well. "She started staying with me to get away from the pressure at home and let herself heal. Her dad inferred we were sleeping together. You should have seen how happy he was." Alex shook his head in disgust. "I was already being groomed for a position within Keane Industries. Then he came down with his ultimatum. Sara Beth was devastated."

And why wouldn't she be? Her own father hadn't cared about her personal happiness so much as what he deemed was best for the company's future.

"So you got engaged. Then what?"

"We held firm as long as we could, hoping the engagement would appease him. Sara Beth had been rising steadily within the company, learning from the ground up after graduating from business school, but when your father doesn't want you in a position of authority, it's the ultimate glass ceiling."

Cailin's voice held a mix of understanding and shock. "He would promote you but not his own daughter?" His chin bumped her head when he nodded, and Cailin asked, "How did she end up in charge of the development department then?"

Bitterness rose at the memory. "He agreed to make me senior VP upon our marriage."

"And in that position, he couldn't block you from promoting her yourself."

"Exactly. We married and moved to Atlanta, and here we are. Sara Beth's work in development has caught the notice of some key board members. Eventually we hope to persuade them to make her my equal when John retires, allowing us to run the company jointly."

Cailin soothed him with quiet strokes along his thigh. "And in the meantime, you're stuck in a holding pattern."

"Yeah. Over time we realized what deep shit we were in. The reality of keeping such a big secret hit hard, but we managed. It helped that Sara Beth had Sam. They're committed partners. She didn't have to worry about being alone."

"Not like you did." Cailin squirmed, demanding his touch, and he realized his hand had stilled on her belly.

"Yeah," he said again. Tucking his other arm under her neck, he pulled her back against him, holding his miracle in his arms. "Then you came along."

"But what if I hadn't? Were you—" The muscles under his hand tightened. "You plan to run the company together. Are you just planning to stay married forever?"

His sigh ruffled her curls. "With my move into the senior VP position, we thought I might be entrenched enough that an amicable divorce would still enable the two of us to fill our positions after John retired. But—"

"But what?"

"But lately John's been demanding other things."

"Like?"

He braced himself. "Like an heir."

"Oh."

That one soft sound conveyed more pain than he'd thought possible. Which was why he hadn't brought it up yet. When they'd agreed to commit only to each other—odd for a married man to say to anyone besides his wife, but there it was—Cailin had told him about her infertility so they wouldn't have to continue using condoms. Alex still didn't know how he felt about having kids, but he knew he wanted Cailin in his life, in his arms, and if she couldn't have kids, hell, maybe they'd eventually adopt. Whatever they needed to do. A couple didn't have to be married to build a family together, however they chose to do so.

That didn't mean another woman carrying his biological child wouldn't be a hard blow.

Finally she asked, "Would you...do that?"

"We've talked about me being a donor for Sara Beth and Sam before. Now? I really don't know."

Silence settled between them once more. Alex didn't break it, wanting to give Cailin a chance to digest everything. Instead he threw his leg over both of hers, surrounding her, reinforcing with his body what he'd already begun to realize in his heart: he'd never leave her.

Finally Cailin stirred. In a low, tender voice she said, "I think that would be very special."

His eyes closed at the powerful surge of emotion in his chest, an emotion he finally allowed himself to acknowledge: love. He loved this woman. She amazed him. She touched something in him that he'd kept hidden from the world. She gave selflessly; he couldn't imagine more courage, more strength than he saw in her heart.

And he couldn't tell her.

As things stood, he could not be wholly hers. And as certain as he was in that moment that his heart would forever belong to her, he refused to shackle her to him, not with the reality that she could be waiting five, even ten years. No, it had to be her choice: stay or go. Always hers. Because she deserved more than the love of a married man.

Cailin turned her face up to his. "Hey," she said with a frown. A fingertip swiped at his cheek, and Alex realized it was wet—and so were his eyes. "What is it?"

He shook his head and locked down his emotions. "You. Just you."

Turning completely to face him, Cailin smiled. "You too."

∞

The courtyard across the street from the Hermitage teemed with life. For the entire city block, a long square cobblestone area stretched, spotted with park benches, leafy trees, and dozens of people, most of whom were hurrying in one direction or another. Fancy dress clothes mixed with nightclub stretch minis and casual shorts and tennis shoes. This part of downtown Nashville was central to many of the area's attractions, and Cailin could have sat all day just people watching, especially if Alex was there, just like he was now, sitting against her on the bench, openly holding her hand.

Women—far too many women—stared as they walked past. In a business suit and tie, Alex commanded the attention of all who saw him. In tight jeans and cowboy boots? He made women melt and men wish they were him. At least they should, considering not one woman paid attention to anyone else when they saw him. A smug smile tilted her lips. They could stare all they wanted; he was hers.

"What's that look all about?"

Cailin tilted her head toward Alex. The view was even better up close, not that she'd share it with anyone. Since he discovered that the feel of his soft black stubble against her skin caused her to squirm—in a good way—Alex had decided not to shave this weekend. His neglected beard gave him a sweaty-cowboy-calendar look that made her feel like she needed to be hosed off. It was irresistible, as evidenced by the fact that it was seven thirty in the evening on Saturday and they'd ventured out of their hotel room—heck, out of their bed—for the first time only an hour ago. Dinner in the hotel's restaurant, for which they were seriously underdressed, and then they'd walked across to the courtyard for what Alex would only describe as a "surprise." As it was, Cailin hadn't been sure she would manage the trip across the road, her legs were so wobbly. She no longer wondered what a real, romantic honeymoon would be like; Alex had shown her everything she'd wanted to know and more.

"Just enjoying the fresh air," she said. Alex's quirked brow shouted *liar!* but no way was she telling him she was gloating in her ownership. Some things were better kept secret, like her alphabet of sins.

They're my *dirty little secrets. Why can't I at least enjoy one or two?*

Alex hummed thoughtfully. Then, affecting a truly excruciating German accent, he said, "We have ways of making you talk, you know."

Laughter bubbled up in her chest. "Oh really? I think I'd like to see some of those. Later." She winked.

Alex's laugh was muffled between their lips as they shared a not so quick kiss. It felt positively wicked to be out in the open, enjoying him, away from the restrictions that ruled their every moment together back in Atlanta. No worries, no limits, only the two of them and—

Alex pulled back to look around the courtyard. "Ah, here she is," he said.

Cailin turned to glance in the same direction. A woman in a floor-length red dress walked carefully across the cobblestones in the darkening twilight, headed their way, swinging a lit lantern in one hand. Cailin did a double take, realizing the dress had to be a replica of an eighteenth- or nineteenth-century walking costume. The long, slightly puffed sleeves must be excruciating considering the air was only now cooling, bringing the temperature into the upper eighties, but the woman seemed oblivious to the heat. What the heck was she doing here, though? And why was Alex looking for her?

Several of the surrounding benches had filled as they sat, and now the woman wandered into their midst and, incongruously, raised a cell phone in one hand. "Anyone here for the ghost tour?"

"Wait here, hon," Alex said to Cailin. "I'll get us checked in."

137

Cailin literally bounced on the seat. "That's us? We're going—"

"Yeah. A ghost tour of downtown Nashville. Sound like fun?"

"Yes!" She reached up and dragged his face down to meet hers for an enthusiastic smack of lips. "Thank you. I can't wait."

Alex laughed. "Well, you'll have to wait until I get us checked in."

"Oh, right." Cailin snatched her hands back quickly. Alex chuckled, gave her another swift peck, then walked over to talk to their hostess for the tour.

By the time Alex returned to their bench, she'd managed to stop bouncing from excitement, but her smile was so wide her cheeks ached. A hint of teasing coloring his voice, he nudged her shoulder and asked, "So it's a walking tour. Think you're up to it?"

A blush heated her cheeks at the thought of her earlier complaints. Alex laughed and settled in behind her, his chest a solid wall of support, until their guide called them to gather around for the beginning of the tour.

"Good evening. I'm Mary," she said. "Welcome to the Music City Downtown Ghost Tour. We've got lots of spooky stuff for you to see tonight, so get your walking shoes on and let's get going. Follow me."

Their first stop was across from the elegant cream-and-black facade of the Hermitage Hotel, where Mary sent shivers down Cailin's spine as she shared stories about the ghosts seen and ghostly noises heard throughout the hotel. As darkness settled around them, they continued their slow walk down the street, past the Tennessee Performing Arts Center, where crowds milled to see the latest offering by the theater, and various empty office buildings while Mary filled them in on the history of Nashville and its early years as an important river port for the South. By the time they reached the end of Sixth Avenue, it was full dark and the State Capitol Building loomed directly ahead.

Staring at the up-lit structure built atop a bow-backed hill, she could see why people would expect to find ghosts here. There was something eerie about the heavily columned building, at least at night, especially with the surrounding grounds, heavily planted with gardens and trees, dark. Mary's story about rival architects buried together inside the capitol building didn't help.

"Spooky," Alex whispered in her ear. His warm breath sent a shiver along her spine that had nothing to do with ghosts. As they crossed the street, she wished for a moment that they'd stayed in the hotel room, where she could have followed up on that shiver. When they took the first set of stairs toward the top of the hill, the darkness drove her closer to Alex, clinging to his broad, strong hand, and the resulting tingle gave her a totally different—and totally naughty—idea.

The group spread out to explore the area around the building, many heading toward the lighted side near President James K. Polk's tomb. Alex stepped in that direction, but Cailin inhaled a deep breath, took a chance, and tugged him in the other. Barely visible, a hedge of evergreens lined the front area, providing a small alley of privacy she hoped to take advantage of.

"Where are we—"

Cailin used a fingertip to stop Alex's question. Instead she drew him behind the evergreens, standing at least ten feet tall, backed him into the fragrant wall, and sank hastily to her knees.

"Cailin?"

Fingers trembling at the audacity of what she was about to do—and at the overwhelming desire to do it—Cailin reached up and placed both hands on Alex's crotch. He choked even as his length hardened beneath her touch. The power she seemed to hold over his body awed her. Right now she'd use it to her advantage, for his pleasure.

Knowing seconds counted, she opened the button of his jeans by shoving her hands under his untucked button-down and giving a single flick to the top button. She didn't even bother to lower the zipper all the way, just lowered it enough to maneuver the head of his shaft through the gap. His breathing bellowed in her ears, his pulse jumped between her fingers, and her mouth watered as she opened enough to take him in.

Fast. Frantic. She poured everything she had into pleasuring him, needing only the taste of his release on her tongue to satisfy her. She couldn't tell if the sounds Alex was emitting were laughter or sobs. Either way, minutes later he was exploding in her mouth, his hands clutching her hair as he strained to empty every last drop into the moist cavern surrounding him. His salty release hit her tongue, and molten pleasure blinded her for long moments. Only Alex's pulling back and the slide of his cock from her mouth returned her to the present.

"God, Cailin," Alex said, strangled laughter making his words choppy, "what was that about?"

Standing, she helped him straighten his clothes until he was as presentable as they could make him in the almost nonexistent light. "It's about surprising you," she replied.

"I'd surprise you too, but I don't think we have time for me to reciprocate."

"Don't have to. This tour was gift enough. Thank you," she whispered as the sound of the others approaching filtered through the trees.

"You're welcome, and yes, I do. And I will." A hard, thorough kiss, then, "Just you wait."

Cailin had a feeling the rest of the tour would be a blur with that promise ahead of her. She was right. Though a crowd of people surrounded them, somehow the sensations Alex conjured overwhelmed her senses. He led her down the street in their guide's wake, his knowing fingers trailing along the valley that bisected her back and sending shivers—the good kind—down her spine. Goose bumps pebbled her skin as Alex stood behind her in Painter's Alley, her bare neck sensitive to the lingering of his breath against it. St. Mary's and the story of the priest found inside its walls made nothing more than a vague impression as Alex's hands molded her hips, kneading, rubbing, sometimes dipping low—and behind—to distract her from every word. And boldest of all, the press of his fingers against the sides of her aching breasts, already tender and throbbing from the attention he'd lavished on them all weekend, as they lingered in the darkened parking lot outside the famous Ryman Auditorium.

Cailin's senses were drunk on Alex; there was no need to visit one of the many bars that waited at the end of the tour. Instead a rushed good-bye and "thank you so much" for their guide, and they were hurrying back to the hotel, anxious for each other and nothing else. No one else. Just the two of them, lost in a world of their own making. Lost in the hunger they had for each other, a hunger the "real world" would have them deny.

∞

Sunday morning, the sun brought reality home to Cailin. She woke, safe and warm, the heavy weight of Alex's arm and leg thrown over her body. She snuggled against him, the feel of his crisp chest hair abrading her back evoking a tenderness she'd never experienced before. Evoking something else she wanted to deny but couldn't: love.

She loved him. The thought struck like lightning there in the quiet of a perfect, peaceful new day. It stunned her. It overwhelmed her. And as amazing as it was, as quick as it had been, it just felt right.

In the short two months since they'd first met, she knew Alex better—his body, his emotions, the way his mind worked—than she'd ever known her ex-husband. Tears pooled. Though she'd tried, there had been nothing she could do to save her marriage. You couldn't know someone who didn't want you to know them, or to know you. Alex shared himself wholeheartedly, both in bed and out. He healed her; loving him healed her. She felt whole. Happy.

Hungry.

But reality hit when she sat up. The first thing she saw turned out to be her suitcase, waiting on the luggage rack. Today she would fill it, pack up the clothes and memories and happiness, and head back to Atlanta, where Alex didn't belong to her but to Sara Beth. Where their relationship hid in the shadows and every kiss, every touch was furtive. Alex had told her that living with the secret would be hard; she hadn't understood exactly how hard it would be until now, until she'd tasted the freedom of living without it and realized how she truly felt about him.

It was the love she now recognized that would help her do whatever it took to stay with him, secrets or not. Amid that alphabet of sins, she had to have some good traits, right? Well, strength was one of them. Determination. They would make it. They'd figure out something.

"We will, I promise." Alex's breath hit her shoulder a moment before his lips.

"Will what?"

"Figure something out."

"Oh." She hadn't realized she'd spoken aloud. "I guess…"

Alex rubbed his chin lightly along her shoulder. "I know Sara Beth and I didn't exactly think this thing through, but that doesn't mean we can't figure it out." Tugging her around, he looked solemnly into her eyes. "I want to be with you, Cailin. Only you. Just be patient, please."

Cailin nodded, but already the heaviness had settled over her. The next few months, possibly years, would be hard. She just prayed she had the strength and determination she thought she did.

Chapter Eleven

Alex rushed into the office early Monday morning, anxious to see Cailin after their night apart, only to be brought up short at the sight that greeted him.

"About time you showed up," John Keane stated sourly as he stood at the window opposite Cailin's desk, the backlight giving his military-cut white hair a totally inappropriate halo. One glance showed Cailin pale and trembling. Shit. John had obviously been his usual charming self, and there was no way to comfort her. John would notice. The man didn't miss anything.

"John, what are you doing in Atlanta?"

"Working, unlike you. Heard you took the weekend off. What the hell were you thinking, gallivanting off for the weekend with the consortium less than four weeks away? If you weren't my son-in-law, I'd fire your ass."

Alex forced himself not to do anything disrespectful like roll his eyes. Instead he ushered the older man into his office, returning to give Cailin a frantic request to call Sara Beth in and a look of sympathy that was far too short before returning to contain the problem as best he could.

"So where were you?" John asked.

Alex bit his tongue, forcing himself to silence.

"Hmm." John's gaze could level entire armies, but Alex stood firm against it. Then, "It's not a woman, is it?"

"God, John. Sara Beth is your daughter. I love her."

John harrumphed again, his expression skeptical. "And you've had her far more than the six months you've been married. A man has needs; I know. I am one. But you've never disappointed me, Alex. Don't start now, especially not over a hot piece of ass."

Choking on the need to strangle his father-in-law, Alex counted slowly to ten; then, when he could get the words out without the urge to kill being obvious, he said, "John, you're going to keep talking, and we're going to have words. You've been like a father to me"— *a really bad one*—"so for both our sakes, shut up."

Anger lit the green eyes so like Sara Beth's, though their personalities were miles apart. Something in Alex's expression must have gotten through, however, because John subsided just as the office door opened and Sara Beth hurried in.

"Dad, what are you doing here?"

"Why the hell is everyone asking me that? He isn't president yet, for Christ's sake," John grumbled, pointing at Alex. "You'd think I wasn't wanted in my own company."

No, just not in this office. Why do you think we moved so far away?

"Of course you're wanted." Sara Beth enveloped John in a warm hug, her generous spirit reaching out to her father in the way only Sara Beth had. Over her shoulder, Alex stared daggers at John, daring him to hurt the woman he held in his arms.

Letting go of her father, Sara Beth stepped immediately to Alex's side, tucking herself under his arm. Her body trembled against him, squeezing his heart. He'd always hated the way John treated her, the conflict it created. She needed the man's approval in some deeply hidden part of herself, the same way all people searched, sometimes fruitlessly, for the approval of their parents. That John would never truly grant that approval was a given; Sara Beth accepted it, and so did Alex. It didn't stop that little-girl part of her from surfacing in John's presence.

Pleasantries were lost on John; they both knew it, but Sara Beth tried anyway. After learning the weather in California was miserably hot and no one they'd known there was worth remembering, she gave up. With only a slight look of exasperation—which was amazing in itself—Sara Beth offered a tour. "You haven't seen the new offices yet. Let me show them to you."

John was already shaking his head. "Alex and I have work to do." When she opened her mouth to speak, he cut her off. "Nothing to worry your pretty little mind about. Alex can give me a tour while we talk." A head jerk indicated the door. "You run along, now."

Alex braced himself against the fury surging inside. It didn't do any good. John had long ago made his thought process clear: Sara Beth was a means to secure the company with a good man, nothing more. Trying to prove she was anything else was just beating their heads against a wall.

But knowing it didn't stop Alex from getting angry. Or Sara Beth.

Her beautiful mouth tightened into a thin line of hurt and resentment. "What am I, twelve?"

Hmm, intervene or not? Nothing she said would affect John; the man's heart seemed to be made of

Teflon, if it even existed at all. Sara Beth, on the other hand...

Sara Beth interrupted before he could decide. "You do realize you sent me to a renowned business school—a very expensive renowned business school, by the way—to earn a top-notch degree to help run this company. I know our work as well as Alex does. There's nothing we don't discuss, no secrets in how we do things here."

Alex nodded. That was how they rolled. Not only was it the fair thing to do, but Sara Beth had a great head for business, one he would never neglect to make use of even if she hadn't been the owner's daughter.

The pain in her words might kill him, though. Her voice actually cracked as she told John, "I'm the fucking head of your development department. Alex recognizes my value. When will you?"

A crease appeared between John's eyebrows. "Alex is your husband. He will run this company. There's a reason you married, remember."

"Maybe I should quit then," she said, throwing her hands up in the air. "My work here is obviously done. I've spread my legs for a man. Whoopie."

"Are you sure you're not pregnant? You're emotional enough to be." Ignoring Sara Beth's shocked gasp, he continued. "And if you're not, maybe home is exactly where you need to be. You're obviously not spending enough time with those legs spread if you're not breeding yet."

"John!" Alex roared, unable to take any more. A single threatening step forward had John eyeing him warily. "Let me make myself perfectly clear. Talk to her like that again, and you can shove this company up your tight ass."

Rage shimmered through him, only Sara Beth's tiny, trembling white hand on his chest holding him back from tearing her father to pieces. Yes, he knew people depended on them; they weren't more important than Sara Beth. He would never allow her to live with those kinds of insults again. It was why he'd married her, why they'd moved. Everything else was secondary.

Without a word, Sara Beth gathered herself, then turned for the door. One hand on the knob, she flung a final look at her father over her shoulder. Pain stared out from her eyes, a pain Alex knew was slowly turning to hatred. Her father didn't see it, never would, but Alex could. The thought of Cailin, her eyes shadowed this morning, slipped into his mind. How much longer could they all do this?

"I'll see you this evening, love," he told her, silently urging her to go.

A careful nod and Sara Beth slipped out the door. John's sigh was loud in the ensuing silence. Shaking his carefully styled white head, he said, "I still wish she'd been a man."

And we all wish you were too, John. Unfortunately we don't always get what we want.

"So," the older man said, "what's the problem with Ian? Why aren't we ready to go? Take me to the man's office. He obviously needs someone to light a fire under his ass."

He's not the only one.

∞

Sara Beth's fingers were nimble on his bow tie. Alex had never gotten the hang of tying the damn things, so he always left the job to her. Tonight, though, he wished it were Cailin's hands on the piece of black silk around his neck.

Sara Beth patted his clean-shaven cheek. "There you go. All set."

Alex's response strongly resembled a grunt.

"Oh hush." A frown marred the smooth skin of Sara Beth's expressive face. "I think we're both suffering from a lack of…"

"A definite lack," he agreed. With John staying here at the house, neither Sara Beth nor Alex had spent significant time with their other half. Sam couldn't stay overnight, and the possibility of making it to Cailin's with John watching his every move was nigh on impossible. The lack of relief—and comfort—added to the edge John brought to every encounter, meant they were both strung pretty tight. Fortunately the man was scheduled to return to California tomorrow. If not, Alex and Sara Beth might be forced to implement one of the fantasies they'd dreamed up in the long week past—fantasies involving John and an unmarked grave somewhere extremely remote.

"At least she'll be here tonight," Sara Beth said. The dinner party John had planned for his last night in town included a host of muckety-mucks from Atlanta's top companies. Anything to increase profits and networking. The possibility of any wheeling and dealing turning serious meant Cailin would be here, available for any "little jobs" John might think up. And while he didn't like having her in the same room as his father-in-law, Alex wanted her here with an intensity that rattled his bones.

Brushing a soft kiss along the corner of Sara Beth's mouth in thanks for the reminder, he turned to grab the tux laid out on his bed. The noose around his neck tightened as he shrugged into the thing. Holy fuck. This week from hell could not be over soon enough.

"Ready?" Sara Beth asked.

Alex grimaced but took her arm anyway. They moved toward the door, the silk of Sara Beth's floor-length gown whispering against his trouser leg with every step.

"You are one fine escort tonight, love," Alex told her, holding his bedroom door open. "It's hard to believe so much beauty could go hand in hand with so much brains. I'm very lucky."

"Why yes, yes, you are." Sara Beth's smile was the first genuine one he'd seen all week. The need to kill John rose, more vicious than ever.

The spiral staircase leading into the grand foyer always gave him a bit of a headache. All those gleaming surfaces: banisters, wood, mirrors, marble tiles... Neither Sara Beth nor he had really wanted such a showcase for a home, but John had insisted. *You're going to be entertaining. Your position in this company demands it, Alex.* They'd managed to avoid entertaining at home until now. The comfortable den at the back of the second-story apartment was the most used room, along with the kitchen and their bedrooms. The rest? Just empty space for their housekeeper to come in and dust once a week. Taking a look around, he couldn't help wondering what Cailin would think. Did she know him well enough to understand how much of this was just show, how much he and Sara Beth hid beneath the surface? Eyeing the massive crystal chandelier hanging low above the entryway, he knew she did. She understood him, inside and out. She wouldn't mistake this place for being a reflection of his true personality.

John wandered out from the sitting room, a glass tumbler of amber liquid in one hand. "About time." His wiry white eyebrows wrinkled as he inspected the two of them, finally giving a reluctant nod of approval. When the doorbell rang, Alex felt Sara Beth's sigh of relief. The less time she spent as the focus of her father's attention, the better.

Guests arrived, one after another. The volume rose as couples mixed and mingled. Along with her inherent talent for business, Sara Beth liked people, and it showed in her hostessing skills. Alex was thankful; he'd rather slit his throat than attend, much less host, one of these gatherings. John's overbearing personality more than made up for Alex's shortfall in that area, however. By the time Cailin arrived, his lone presence in the foyer made for sweet relief.

Opening the door, Alex stood and stared, his breath frozen. Cailin held out her hands from her sides, offering herself for inspection as she waited on the front steps. The movement showcased her delectably feminine figure, outlined to perfection in candy-red chiffon. The dress reminded him of red hots, so much so that his mouth watered. Material lovingly draped her round breasts, slinked along her nipped-in waist, and parted provocatively at midthigh to reveal Marilyn Monroe legs he desperately needed wrapped around him soon. Thank God for the tux, which helped cover an instant erection he couldn't have stopped without medical intervention. And when she turned to close the door behind herself, he almost swallowed his tongue.

"Oh God."

Cailin peeked over her shoulder and grinned. The bare expanse of silky-smooth skin from her neck to her tailbone gleamed in the overhead light. "Like it?" she whispered huskily.

Since all the spit in his mouth had dried up, Alex could only nod, his gaze glued to the tiny dimples winking on either side of the barely visible tops of her perfect ass cheeks. Damn.

"Where the hell did you find that dress?" he asked huskily.

"Oh, ask Sara Beth." Cailin turned, her breasts jiggling lightly in a way that drew his attention immediately—and probably every other guy in the place as soon as they saw them. "I'm sure she'll take me back if you like this one."

"Uh-huh." Fascination rose as her nipples visibly peaked beneath the soft material. The urge to find a shawl, towel, blanket—anything—and hide her in it almost overwhelmed him. He drew a shaky hand down his face.

"Alex. What the hell are you doing lollygagging in here? Come mingle, for God's sake."

John's voice jerked Alex out of the haze enveloping him. He didn't miss the softening of Cailin's nipples as her desire fled. The rest of her body tensed.

"Um, why don't you go ahead? I'll stay and answer the door if anyone else arrives."

He nodded before glancing out of the stained-glass side light. "There are only two we're missing now." Turning back, he fought not to get lost in her eyes again. "Be sure and come in when they do."

"Alex!"

The tiny flinch of Cailin's body made him want to throw something. "I'll see you in a few minutes," he told her.

She nodded, hastily turning toward the front door. He wished he could escape so easily.

John hauled him aside before Alex could enter the main living room. The man's grip on his tux was ruthless, demanding Alex's attention. "It's the secretary, isn't it? You're fucking your secretary."

A hot burst of rage lit his mind. Sparing a glance over his shoulder to make certain Cailin was out of range of his father-in-law's accusations, he clamped down hard on his tongue and forced himself to silence. Denying he was sleeping with anyone but his wife wouldn't make a bit of difference to John, even if Alex could have lied with such blatancy. Instead he simply stared at John and let the man dig his own hole.

"As much as I love Sara Beth"—at John's words, Alex bit into the tender muscle in his mouth so hard blood surged into his throat—"a man has his needs. But a secretary?" Disgust colored the word. "That's just cliché."

"She's my executive assistant, John. Get with the times."

"Exec—" An impatient flick of his hand. "Whatever. She's a woman, an available woman if her naked ring finger is the truth, not that it always is. But regardless, you don't piss in your own watering hole. If you need a little something on the side, do what we always did: keep them in an apartment somewhere, far away. Not in the office."

As if Cailin were a two-bit whore Alex just played around with. "I never said I was sleeping with her."

"But you looked at her."

Shit! Was it that obvious? John was astute, but so were many of the men he worked with. Had he put the woman he loved in that precarious a position? "So? A man can look." He threw a nod over his shoulder, knowing Cailin was visible as she stood at the front door, looking out onto the driveway. "Wouldn't you?"

John's eyes on his woman made bile rise in Alex's throat. "Of course I did," John said. "And when you've done your duty by Sara Beth and provided an heir, you can look—and touch—all you want. But. Not. At. The. Office."

"Fuck off, John." Before he said anything else he'd regret, Alex walked into the living room. Away from his father-in-law. Away from the urge to kill. And away from the fear that Cailin might one day see their situation with the very same unrosy glasses.

∞

After dinner Cailin slipped out of the formal dining room, needing desperately to catch her breath. Finding a bathroom was at the top of her list as well. Ignoring the caterers whizzing in and out, she wandered up the hall toward the front door, then made her way upstairs.

The expanse of the house amazed her. Considering Alex and Sara Beth lived here alone, the size seemed decadent, but the decor shouted loud and clear *I'm for show*, so the extra square footage didn't surprise her. She figured it was just one more thing the two of them hadn't really had much choice about.

The thought seriously depressed any party mood she might have felt.

The first few rooms she peeked into had *guest room* written all over them. Toward the back of the house, a secure door separated the front from what she assumed was the apartment Sara Beth had mentioned earlier when she passed Cailin the key. Unlocking the heavy door, Cailin slipped through— and walked into another world.

Here, all the warmth absent downstairs came alive. This was where Sara Beth and Alex really lived. The first room was a den, with dark, cushiony furniture, a massive big-screen TV, and all the comforts of a real home. Farther down, a small kitchen opened off the hall. A room that must be Sara Beth's came next, and Cailin couldn't help the surge of relief at the sheer femininity of the decor. Not a hint of masculinity. Alex was man enough that his mere presence would put a stamp on a place. If he'd lived with Sara Beth in this room, Cailin would know. And though he'd told her they slept in separate rooms, always had, some small, uncertain part of her had wondered if that was really true. Turned out it was.

Breathing deep, she closed the door and moved to the end of the hall. Opening the last door, Cailin felt Alex's presence reach out and grab her immediately. She stepped into what had to be his bedroom, judging by the enormous bed that took center stage. Navy and chocolate, gray and cream blended into a visual display of Alex's personality: easygoing and mellow, yet intense, deep. Alex, in all his glorious contradictions, could be felt within these walls.

Walking across the room, Cailin took a moment to make herself at home in the lavish bathroom that made her positively green with envy before coming back out to lie on the soft down comforter, luxuriating in the heavy embrace of Alex's masculine scent. Bits of woodsy musk and lime teased her nose, and memories of the many places on his body where that scent hid rose to taunt her, causing shivers deep in her lower belly. God, she missed him. The week had been empty, just like her bed. She needed him as much as Sara Beth did, only in a different way.

"Hey, you." The low words came around the slightly opened door.

Cailin gasped, jumping off the bed as if it were on fire. "Crap!" Hand over her barreling heart, she glared at Samantha. "What the heck are you doing here?"

Sam came in and closed the door. "I sneaked in a few minutes ago," she said, chuckling. "Since I don't have to be at work tomorrow, I can hide out in Sara Beth's room until dear old Dad heads for the airport. Sara Beth and I couldn't..." She ran a hand through her prettily mussed hair. "We don't like being apart this long."

Cailin nodded. She and Alex were discovering the very same thing. "So there's no risk of John coming back here?"

Sam grinned. "Not with Sara Beth's door locked. She and I have the only keys." A twinkle lit her eye. "We plan to hide it later tonight and play Find the—"

"Whoa!" Cailin could feel her face flushing crimson to match her dress. "TMI, my friend."

Sam's full laughter bellowed out. Cailin joined in, and the two of them piled onto the love seat in the corner of Alex's room together. Rolling her neck, Cailin sighed before lolling her head on the back cushion, facing Sam. "How do you do this?" she asked the other woman.

"You just do. If you love them, you do whatever it takes and know that, in the end, it will be worth it."

"Will it?" Cailin asked softly. She let the heaviness that had slowly been enveloping her as she walked through Alex and Sara Beth's house come out in her voice. "All this"—she waved a hand to indicate the room—"this is their home. The life they've built together." It was a powerful mirage, one that almost had Cailin convinced that nothing she and Alex created would ever be as good. "How do you handle knowing she's connected to him at that level, a level you're denied, even though she loves you?"

Samantha's eyes conveyed her understanding. "I don't really know that I handle it. It just is. Sara Beth brings me into that life as much as she can, but it is what it is. John's not gonna change. Now that you've met him, you must see that."

Just the thought of Sara Beth's father made her tremble harder than the fire-and-brimstone preachers that used to visit her parents' church at revival time. "No, he's not."

"This house is just a product of their love for one another," Sam said. "Neither of them had any siblings, so this is where they've built their 'real' family. Here they are brother and sister, even though the world sees them as a couple. It's no different than

157

me sharing an apartment with my brother, really." Sam shrugged again, and Cailin had the feeling she did that a lot here, as if unconsciously forcing the situation to roll off her back. "When you look at it that way, it gets easier to handle. Knowing that when they touch, it's platonic, not sexual. Sara Beth confessed to me once that they'd tried to…um…have sex." She quirked a brow as if waiting for Cailin to blow up. For some reason Cailin didn't see the need, especially when Sam smirked. "She said it was pretty bad when neither one of them could get excited—a double disaster, she called it."

Cailin grinned at the image too.

Sam's tone sobered. "I admire them both. Sara Beth—she's extraordinary. The things that man has put her through… And yet she's present, she's right there, wholeheartedly, in every moment."

"You love her," Cailin murmured.

"Yes, just like you do Alex."

The words jolted her. "I—"

Nothing else came out. Loving Alex was the only thing she knew with certainty. Nothing she'd ever felt in her life had been like this. But something held her back. Committing to a man—and admitting she loved him was a commitment—was scary enough. Committing to a married man—that was terrifying. What her heart knew and her mouth could say wrangled in her throat, each wanting the upper hand. Neither won.

Sam reached out and patted Cailin's hands as they twisted in her lap. "I know the feeling." Standing, she slapped her jean-clad thighs. "And now, you better get back down there before someone notices your extended absence."

With a deep sigh, Cailin agreed. But when she reached the doorway, she turned back to face the woman trailing her. Her heart thumped painfully. Not knowing what to say, she stood for a moment, gripping the door frame. Finally she went with, "Thank you."

"You're welcome," she said, giving Cailin a hug. "Anytime." She headed into the hall and disappeared into Sara Beth's room.

An hour later, guests began to filter out the front door. Cailin was helping Sara Beth clean up when Alex stopped behind her. "Going straight home?" he asked in a rough whisper.

"Yeah." She wiped a hand across her damp brow. "I'm tired."

"Okay." He ducked his chin. White teeth worked his bottom lip, a sure sign something was on his mind. Cailin waited, knowing he'd get it out when he was ready.

She went back to stacking cups. When she stood, Alex finally said, "I'll be over in a little while."

A frisson of conflicting emotions zipped through her body. "What? But I thought…"

The bitter smile didn't reach Alex's eyes. "I've been given permission to have my cake and eat it too, so to speak."

Cailin's stomach churned at the implications. "John?"

He nodded.

Horror raised the volume of her voice. "He's her"—Alex's abrupt slash of a hand made her lower the volume to a raspy whisper—"her father. God, Alex. That's…" What the hell did she say to that?

She'd thought her parents were bad for cutting her off when she'd divorced, but this—

"Not for her to know," he finished with an arch look.

Cailin agreed hastily. No way would she hurt her friend by even hinting at such a thing.

"Cailin."

She looked up, seeing the strain on Alex's face. The need to touch him, to soothe that hurt, clenched in her gut. "Come."

Pain stared out of his eyes, and though she loved that he wasn't the silent type, that he didn't hide his emotions from her, she hated seeing it. "Are you sure?" he asked.

"Just come," she replied. Hurrying toward the downstairs kitchen was the only thing that kept her hands off him.

Chapter Twelve

Alex wanted desperately to close his eyes to the ugly reality that was his life, but that was difficult to do when he was trying to see in the dark. The step up to Cailin's porch almost tripped him, but he caught himself at the last minute. The need to see her was like craving a drug—it made his hands shake, fogged his vision, created a skip in his heartbeat that had no relation to the pleasant stutter most people associated with love. This wasn't pleasant; it wasn't even really love, not right at the moment. It was simple, painful, overpowering need. No one, nothing else could cleanse the emotions tearing him up inside.

Nothing could make this situation right. Even when the board voted in their favor, sometime down the road, the memories would still be there. The things John had said and done could not be erased, not even with the fulfillment of Sara Beth's dream. That ugliness would always remain, in her mind and his. But for a few minutes, for just a little while, Cailin could take him out of this world and replace reality with the fantasy. That's what he craved right now. The fantasy world he'd built with her.

She must have been watching for him, because as he raised his hand to knock, the door creaked open. Cailin stood in the black opening. Her pale skin was bare, beautiful, and he sucked in his breath at the pleasure it evoked. He felt a moment's regret that he wouldn't be removing the red dress tonight; then sheer lust roared through him, and he stepped across the threshold, slammed the door shut, and grabbed the vision awaiting him.

There was no finesse, no foreplay, only harsh grunts and groans, ripping and tearing, and finally the sheer bliss of Cailin's warm, soft, wet body surrounding his cock. He pushed deep, thankful she was ready. Not until he hilted, rocking against the hard ridge of her cervix, did he still. Cailin moaned, her head rolling slowly against the wall behind her, her channel clenching as she adjusted to his size. With desperate whimpers and tiny thrusts, she begged him to move, but Alex shook his head. He wrapped both hands underneath her ass, clenching the cheeks tightly, forcing her fully against him, laid his head against her breastbone, his mouth between the soft, tremulous mounds of her breasts, and breathed her in.

His sanity.

His world.

His miracle.

Finally, arms trembling with her full weight, he stumbled back, adjusted, and carefully lowered her to the ground, never losing the connection between them. Cailin sprawled beneath him, blonde curls fanning out like an angel, her eager body clutching him tightly. Her eyes were mysterious pools of darkness, and yet he felt her stare down deep into the heart of him. Nothing hidden, no shame. Just hunger and heat and need.

He grasped her legs where they tucked around him, pushing her knees out and back toward her chest, opening her completely. One slow withdrawal, her tissues dragging, crying to keep him, and then a hard, quick, heavy thrust all the way in. There was no way to keep him out, no way to control the depth of his penetration, and yet, instead of struggling, Cailin grasped her shins, angling her knees out farther, and pulled back, opening herself even more. Alex looked down at where the two of them were joined. Her beautiful lips stretched tight around his shaft, plain even in the low light, glistening with their juices. Alex placed his thumb in her mouth, felt her tongue lave him, and then moved it to the hard pebble of her clit, right there above where their connection began, and pressed in a slow circle.

Cailin wailed.

Like a knife, the sound pierced the bitter haze that had enveloped him. He wanted to hear it again, to drive away the remaining mist, over and over, until all he could see was Cailin, all he could feel were their bodies, all he could think about was driving her higher.

He set up a rhythm: back, forward, circle, press. Repeat. The rise to climax, fast but not fast enough, was killing him. Cailin tensed even more around him, internal muscles fluttering, her legs shaking, her cries frantic. She arched off the floor, only her shoulders and head remaining, her hips grinding against him. Lungs laboring, he drove them both on, Cailin chanting her need with every thrust. "Come, Alex. Come with me. Please."

Until finally he did. The world sheeted white, oblivion, everything seared in the path of the rushing pleasure overtaking his body and hers. He shouted, one final cry, and all went blissfully black.

∞

Cailin hummed. The office was bright with morning sunshine, and even though it was a Monday morning, the world looked just right to her as long as she stayed away from the floor-to-ceiling windows. She dusted the plant that sat in the corner—she never had figured out what kind it was—before grabbing a bottle of water from the stash in the pantry area and watering it. She'd always like plants, though she had the brownest thumb in Alabama, it seemed. Didn't matter what she planted, it died. Maybe that's why this one had survived her stint in Alex's office—she hadn't planted it.

The thought made her laugh and pat the plant's wide green leaves. Moving on to her desk, she straightened and cleaned and put things away, her usual Monday morning routine. Starting the week with a neat office filled her with anticipation. Last week all she'd been filled with was dread, since John had been waiting when she walked in. But not today. Today would be a good day.

She'd just bent down to grab the files necessary for today's meetings from the filing cabinet's bottom drawer when a heavy hand gripped her hip.

Joy surged as she turned. "Ale—"

"Good morning, Ms. Gray. Or may I call you Cailin?" James Allen stood far too close, his bulk threatening as he ran a calloused finger along a blonde curl that had escaped her morning upsweep with all the bending and stretching.

What the hell is he doing here? Why didn't security call? After the problem with Tammy, Alex had made certain they were notified before Allen was allowed to step foot in the elevator. And now he'd caught her here, in the office, totally alone since Alex had a meeting with Ian and Sara Beth this morning.

Trying desperately to control the panic making it hard to breathe, Cailin attempted to sidle away from his touch, but the man had fingers like a vise. There would be bruises on her hip later. "Mr. Allen, what—"

"And you can call me James. After all"—his slightly bulging eyes leered their way down her body and back up—"I'm hoping to get to know you very well." A fat pink tongue slicked along his lower lip. "Very well, indeed."

Nausea twisted her stomach. She took a single step backward, all the room she had, pressing her body against the filing cabinet and ignoring the dig of a drawer handle in her spine as she sought any way to escape the man's proximity. "I don't understand."

His poor-innocent-me look wasn't innocent at all. "You don't? Well, maybe I can explain it to you." Thick, hard fingers traced the edge of her collarbone above her blouse. Cailin was distinctly aware of the threat of that hand, of how easily it could slip—or shove—below the flimsy material protecting her right now. Automatically her hand flew up, slapping him away. She tore at his fingers on her hip, but the hand she'd slapped tangled in her hair, lifting until she was pulled taut, stretched along the front of the filing cabinet as if it were a rack. The muscles in her legs strained as she went up on tiptoe, trying desperately to release the pull on her hair.

"Uh-uh-uh, naughty girl." Allen's alcohol-laden breath hit with almost as much force as his heavy body slamming her against the cabinet. His fingers tightened cruelly, forcing a gasp from her lips.

"What are you doing? Let go of me!"

He snorted his opinion of that demand. "Don't get so excited, missy. I know what you're here for. I just decided to take advantage of it." His flushed face dipped down, and he drew a deep breath, scenting her like a dog. The nausea rose to the back of her throat. "If I'd known what a hypocrite our Alex was, I'd have had my eye on you a whole lot sooner."

"What are you talking about?"

"Well, see, I took me a trip to Nashville recently."

Her fear-saturated brain struggled to make a connection. *Nashville?* Nashville. Oh God...

She turned her head, straining away from him, panic thumping a heavy drumbeat in her chest. Allen laughed, the sound pouring over her like an oil slick, as he transferred the hand on her hip to her jaw and forced her to face him again. "I see you're getting my drift. I just happened to have tickets for the play downtown. There I am, walking across Sixth Avenue, when I look up and what do I see but little ol' you hanging all over our very own Mr. Alex Holier-than-thou Brannigan. Right there, in the street. As if he wasn't a married man and all."

A tilt of his hips brought a firm bulge in contact with her churning stomach. Pure, electrifying adrenaline shot through her already trembling limbs. "Please..."

She hated the whimpering sound of her own voice. The fact that she and Alex had been seen together didn't even matter right now. Who cared, anyway? Not John, that was for sure. After what that prick had said to Alex, she figured he could have a harem and John wouldn't care as long as he stayed married to Sara Beth and did what was best for the company. No, what mattered was getting out of here without being raped. How the hell had he known she'd be alone?

"Mr. Allen, please, you need to let me go. Alex will be back any—"

"Shut up!" Droplets of spit hit her face with every hard word. "You don't think I'm stupid, do ya? You think I can't get in here anytime I want?" Wet lips left a slimy trail along her cheek as he moved across it to whisper in her ear. "Did you know one of the security officers retired last week? I did. I made sure the most qualified candidate for the job was offered up. Money can open doors—literally." His laugh blasted her ear.

Cailin slid her eyes closed, trying frantically to calm herself, to think. Instead, panic had her struggling against him, desperate to get free, to escape the feel of his body against her. Tears pooled at the pain digging into her spine, in her neck and jaw as she dangled from Allen's relentless grip, but she couldn't stop. She needed to get away.

A yelp slipped out as he yanked her head back hard, and she gave in to anger and adrenaline surging in her system. The time for helplessness and tears was over—it was time to fight. Another jerk threatened to snatch her hair from her scalp. *Damn it!* "Let go!" she shrieked, lifting her foot to kick out at him, but the movement only let him slip between her legs, her heel sliding ineffectually along his shin.

Allen laughed. "You're a feisty one, aren't ya. I like the feisty ones. All piss and vinegar and fire. I was watching you the other night. That sexy red dress." He ground against her. "That round ass." He tilted his head to stare down her blouse. "I bet those are just as round, aren't they? And I'm gonna find out, so don't bother playin' coy with me. We all saw how Alex was looking at you, and you at him. You're just his dirty little secret—and men don't care about their dirty little secrets. Didn't you know that?"

"No." Alex cared; she knew he cared.

"Oh yes." His palm slid from her chin down her body until cruel fingers bit into her breast. "Alex is gettin' too big for his britches. He thinks he can keep his women all to himself, like that silly slut out at reception. He needs to learn a lesson. He needs to realize this is how this company has always run, will always be run"—pain sparked in her breast as he found her nipple and twisted in a cruel pinch—"with or without him. Women have only one role here, and this is it."

From the dark, angry tone of his voice, Cailin knew she was out of time. Allen's patience was at an end, and she might have only one chance to save herself.

Gripping her shirt, Allen stepped back enough to yank down the front, stripping the buttons and opening the flap in one heavy jerk. Taking advantage of the distance between them, she lashed out again, her foot finding his knee with a hard *snap*, her hands aiming for his eyes. She missed, fingernails gouging into his cheeks. Allen howled in rage and backhanded her.

She felt the impact as she hit the side of her desk and rolled onto her stomach, had just enough presence of mind to grip the edges to keep herself from skidding off the side before Allen landed on her back. His weight was like a full-ton bull pinning her down, denying her breath, as he grabbed the hem of her skirt and shoved it upward. Gathering what little air she could, Cailin focused all her strength and let out a scream to rival the best B-movie heroine who ever belted one out on the silver screen.

"Damn, woman!" Allen bent over her, reaching for her mouth, and she forced her head back before she could reconsider. The back of her head met the front of his face, and the distinct *crack* of something hard giving way sickened her. The next moment, his weight was gone, and she could breathe again.

"Alex! Alex!"

Ian's voice confused her. What was he doing here? Where had he come from? But she was too exhausted to care. All the strength she could gather was just enough to slide off the edge of the desk, down onto the floor. Her legs wouldn't hold her. Her brain shut down. Nothing registered except the feel of the solid wood at her side, keeping her from lying down on the rich cushion of the plush carpet beneath her.

"Cailin!" Tammy's voice, concerned, shaken.

"It's all right. I'm all right," Cailin reassured her, not wanting the woman to cry. She didn't even really know what she was saying. All she knew was the hands were gone from her body, and now, in the aftermath, everything was fuzzy.

Thank God.

The next thing she knew, Alex was there, his arms surrounding her, his warmth sustaining her, his touch so very different from Allen's. And God help her, but she was afraid she was going to do a very Southern thing and faint like some Scarlett O'Hara idiot. She fought it, fought the blackness. Instead she focused on dark, dark eyes, letting them fill her world, and waited for everything else to settle into quiet.

∞

Alex was still shaking as he showed the final member of the Atlanta PD out of his office. Who gave a fuck if it made him look weak? The sight of Cailin, pinned under that asshole, struggling to stop him from raping her—it was all he could think about. When he closed his eyes, it was seared into his eyelids. Even with his eyes open, it was hard to concentrate on anything else.

A soft touch on his forearm had him turning back to the room, realizing he was still standing, staring at the door.

"Alex, come sit down," Sara Beth said.

His gaze flicked past her to the couch, where Cailin was huddled in a blanket. One side of her face was beginning to swell; no doubt a black eye would appear before tomorrow. The lump on the back of her head had concerned the EMT, but she'd refused to go to the hospital. From the way she'd shuddered at the slightest touch of anyone but him, Alex figured it was probably revulsion more than thinking she didn't have a concussion that kept her away. He couldn't blame her. She'd had enough hands on her this morning.

He crossed the room to stoop in front of her, lifted her stretched-out legs, and sat, settling her legs across his lap. He kept his touch gentle as he stroked her; the glimpses of the bruises on her thighs when the EMT had examined her earlier demanded it.

Blowing out a heavy sigh didn't relax the tension in his own body, however.

"What's wrong?" she asked.

"Everything."

He turned to find her watching him. A shine gathered in her eyes, tightening his chest.

"I'm sorry," she whispered, her voice still gravelly from screaming for help.

Alex shook his head. "For what?"

"For—" She nodded carefully toward the door to the outer office.

The rage that had finally settled after watching the police take Allen out of here in handcuffs flared again. He reached toward her chin, pain spiking when she flinched away from his touch. He ignored it. Having heard her tell her story to the detective, he knew it was instinctive: Allen had gripped her jaw so hard there where already purple shadows there. Instead he caressed the uninjured side of her face and stared fiercely into her tear-filled eyes. "Don't you tell me you're sorry. You did nothing wrong." He leaned forward and swept his lips gently across her swollen mouth. "I'm so proud of you. You fought." Settling his forehead against hers, he whispered, "You did good, sweetheart."

Swollen lids closed over her anxious eyes, forcing tears to trickle down both cheeks. But the tension that had invaded her body melted like ice cream on hot pavement.

The door opened, and Sam entered. After closing the door carefully, she crossed to stand next to Sara Beth, wrapping her arms around her partner. "Doing okay?" she asked as her gaze swept the three of them.

"As well as can be expected," Sara Beth replied. She leaned heavily into Sam's body. "The detective said they'd get back to us on any further questions tomorrow, but it looks cut-and-dried. I just can't believe... I mean, I know after Tammy...he hated you, but still, to be so blatant."

"He was drunk." Alex had smelled the alcohol on him from a yard away.

"He saw us in Nashville," Cailin said, her eyes still closed.

Alex's gut clenched, and for a moment he thought he'd throw up. He'd hurt Cailin enough; the guilt of knowing being with him had led up to this felt like a two-ton brick on his already heavy chest.

"And he thought you were fair game?" Sara Beth asked incredulously. Her green eyes were almost luminous as she glared at Alex. "Why the hell do we put up with this bastard?"

"Well, we won't anymore. After Tammy, I contacted John, but he insisted Allen be kept on board." His fingers clenched involuntarily around Cailin's calf, causing her to flinch. He soothed her with a careful stroke. "I didn't like it, but there was nothing I could do. Now there is."

"But why?" Sara Beth asked. "The man is obviously abusive toward women. Why would Dad want to keep him as an investor?"

"Money," Sam said as if it were obvious. Which it was, but he hadn't wanted to say it.

John's loyalties had always been clear. Even his own daughter didn't earn the respect and love he had for the company he'd built from the ground up. Alex and Sara Beth both had struggled with the decision to simply leave him to it, to walk away from Keane

Industries, but in the end Sara Beth hadn't been able to sacrifice the company she'd been raised to love and the good of the people who needed the company to survive. So she'd stayed, and Alex had stayed with her.

And the golden noose had tightened every single day around their necks.

"This has to stop."

His words echoed in the silence of the room. When he raised his chin to look at Sara Beth, he saw acceptance staring back at him. It was time.

"Alex."

The rough scrape in Cailin's voice emphasized why he was right. They couldn't let anyone else get hurt. But what could they do? How did you wrestle control from a man who rightfully owned that control, even if he wielded it like a sledgehammer, with no thought to the safety and well-being of those around him?

"Alex." This time her voice was louder, insistent. He turned his head to look at her.

"Something…" She cleared her throat. "Maybe… Something Allen said made me wonder."

"Wonder what?"

She glanced at Sara Beth, caution in her eyes. Red hair flew as Sara Beth shook her head. "Oh no you don't. Out with it. We're not sparing petty feelings anymore, Cailin. No more dancing around." In Sara Beth's voice, he heard the hard edge of determination. "The time for that is long past, girlfriend."

Cailin watched her a moment longer, then nodded. Turning back to him, she said, "When Allen was talking, he said this was how the company was run, that there was only one place for a woman." A shiver shook her frame, and her eyes glazed over as her focus turned inward. "This was how it had always been and always would be. What if—"

His brain ramped up at her words, and he didn't like where it was headed. "What?"

"What if...this isn't the first time?" Cailin rubbed a hand across her swollen cheek. "What if this has happened before?"

"But we'd—" Sara Beth's voice cut off, probably with the same realization he was coming to. She wasn't slow on the uptake, even if John was her father. "God, I think I'm going to be sick."

Sam squeezed her waist and guided her to a seat. "So...are we thinking just Allen, or...?"

A hard lump settled in his throat. "John's in charge. Always has been." And his iron fist wouldn't have let anything slip through his fingers. "The corporate culture of Keane Industries is what he made it. And there are an awful lot of his college buddies, men he's known for years before Sara Beth was born, on the board of directors, investing, filling prominent positions. It's why we knew it would take time to win the board over; we'd have to wait for at least a few to retire." He might just join Sara Beth in being sick. "John would have known, even if he hadn't participated himself."

"But you think he did," Cailin said. It was a statement, not a question.

Thinking back to the night of the party, he considered John's warning. Why push Alex away from his secretary if John didn't uphold the same standard? What would John have done if Cailin had brought a harassment suit against Alex?

"If something went wrong between us and you caused problems, John would have to step in," he mused, working through the scenario in his mind. "How hard would it be for me to tell he'd done this before, either for himself or others? Maybe he didn't want me knowing, guessing. Maybe he wanted to make sure their good-ol'-boy club stayed just that— no new members." His gaze met Sara Beth's. "Members who could use that knowledge against him if they chose to."

Was John the instigator or just the cover-up man? Somehow the latter didn't seem to fit. And when he remembered the way John had stared at Cailin that night, his gaze trailing the bare expanse of her back as she stood in the foyer, Alex knew. He knew, and the knowledge could be what he needed to find a quicker way out of this mess.

"Alex, how…? We can't." Sara Beth swallowed hard enough for him to hear it. "That would be blackmail."

Resolve hardened his words. "Yes, yes, it would." He looked at Cailin again, at her injuries. "And blackmail would be exactly what he deserves. That and a whole lot more."

Chapter Thirteen

Ten days later, Alex was lying on his bed, the stereo on, when Sara Beth knocked on his door. He'd considered going home with Cailin but, after the day they'd had, figured Sara Beth might need him tonight. Apparently he'd been right.

The door opened, and his best friend scampered across the room to pile up next to him. He squeezed her to his side, inhaling the fresh, wild scent of her red hair, and was surprised by a vague sense of regret. It wouldn't be long and these moments would be gone. They would both be holding someone else, and as much as he loved Cailin, Sara Beth had been his anchor for eighteen years. His life would have been far different without her. And after the consortium this coming weekend, everything would change. The thought made him both hungry for Cailin and sad for Sara Beth and himself.

When he chuckled, Sara Beth turned her face toward him. "What's so funny?"

"I was just thinking we're both about to leave the nest. 'Bout time, huh?"

Sara Beth's smile didn't quite reach her eyes. "Yeah, about time." She went back to staring at the ceiling.

He linked his hand with the one resting on her stomach. "I'm sorry about today."

Another one of those unhappy smiles. "Me too. I mean, as much as I'd prepared myself for it to happen, I guess you can't really ever be ready to find out your father's a complete prick, ya know?"

No, he didn't know. But he had seen what the knowledge cost her as they'd talked to Corrine Henderson today. It had been Sara Beth's idea to contact John's longtime secretary. They'd both known it was a risk. There were no guarantees that Corrine would tell them anything, nor that the woman wouldn't run straight back to John. What they hadn't expected was a complete chronicle of the life and times of John's male-only "club." Apparently John was no stranger to blackmail—Corrine had kept her job and protected herself by documenting everything she knew about John's activities. When Sara Beth approached her, she'd practically handed them a gift-wrapped guide to taking John down.

For Alex, it had been like getting bashed over the head with a truckload of bricks; he could only imagine what seeing the proof of her father's depravity had felt like to Sara Beth.

"So many women," Sara Beth murmured. "They deserved better. Better than having their jobs depend on putting out. Better than having sexual harassment charges swept under the rug. I just can't believe... What if it had been me? Would he have turned a blind eye on it then? Would he have actively helped a man who abused me?"

Wasn't that what John had done all along? He hadn't sexually abused Sara Beth, but he'd forced her into a marriage he didn't really care if she wanted, attempted to control her life with bribes and demands, even to the point of pressuring her to have children whether she wanted them or not. The fact that John had both condoned the harassment and actively participated in it didn't surprise Alex in the least.

Not that he'd say any of that to Sara Beth. He had a feeling she already knew it; she didn't need to hear it.

Sara Beth finally turned and buried her face in his T-shirt. "Oh God, Alex, what if this doesn't work?" She began to cry, and the sound of her sobs and the wetness of her tears on his skin tore his heart out.

"It will," he whispered into her hair. *It has to.* The anger he'd fought all day rose to choke him. John had done this, and he had yet to pay. That was Alex's responsibility—Sara Beth, Sam, and Cailin were his to protect, and he wasn't about to fail them. John had a firestorm headed his way, and the satisfaction of bringing the trouble right back to his father-in-law's lap was the only thing that could settle his rage over what they'd discovered today.

Sara Beth's tears finally quieted to sniffles, then silence. When she finally spoke, she sounded more resigned than worried. "Were we wrong?"

"About what?"

"Getting married. Maybe there was something else, some way around it."

"Why would you say that?"

Sara Beth shook her head. "I just can't help thinking about the women they've hurt in the past two years. While I was feeling sorry for myself because I couldn't live openly with Sam, there were women who couldn't even go to work without... I married you to protect these people, and it was all for nothing."

"Not for nothing." His chest ached. "Look at me, Sara Beth." When she lifted her gaze to his, he said, "Hindsight is twenty-twenty; isn't that what they say? You can't fix what you didn't know, didn't even suspect. None of us did." He smoothed her bangs out of her tearstained face. "We did what we knew to do under the circumstances." He thought about something Cailin had said to him the other day. "And honestly, hard as it's been…I would never have traded this time with you." He cupped his hand around her cheek and kissed her, right there on the corner of her mouth, the place she'd dubbed "his spot."

"You have given me so much, love," he told her softly. "Made me a better man. I would not be who I am today if it weren't for you." He willed her to see the truth in his words.

The tiny smile that stretched her lips reached her eyes this time.

"We do what we can do, Sara Beth. That's it. Let the chips fall where they may."

He watched as acceptance settled on her, relaxing her body and the tight grooves around her eyes.

"Thanks, Alex."

"Anytime."

They lay for a long while, sharing the silence, until finally Sara Beth said, "What's next?"

He knew she didn't mean the company; they'd discussed that at length. If she meant personally… "We'll figure it out."

"Yeah, we will. Sam and Cailin have stuck it out this far; they aren't going anywhere."

Alex grunted his response.

Sara Beth looked at him. "What did that mean?"

"Nothing."

Turning, she raised up on her elbow to face him. "Cailin's not going anywhere, is she?"

I hope not. He wouldn't know; he hadn't asked her. Call him a coward, but he'd never asked a woman to marry him when there wasn't a built-in guarantee that she'd accept. And Cailin had more reason than most not to commit after the pain her ex had put her through. Not even under the threat of torture would he have given away his uncertainty where she was concerned.

Apparently he didn't have to. Sara Beth smacked his shoulder. "God, you are such a man!"

He looked down his nose at her. "What? I didn't say anything."

"An *idiotic* man! You can't even see what's right in front of your nose."

"And what's that?"

The sneaky smile he'd learned to be wary of appeared out of nowhere. "You haven't told her, have you?"

"Told her what?"

"That you love her. You haven't said it."

Not to her.

"Jeez, Alex. The woman's been through the wringer, and you're holding out on her?" She propped her chin on her hand. "Trust me, I know women—"

He couldn't hold back a snort that said more clearly than words, *much better than I do.*

Sara Beth rolled her eyes and went right on with her sentence. "And I can tell you for a fact that your woman is head over heels. She'd follow you to hell and back."

"She already has," he said.

"So what are you holding out for?"

He swallowed hard, but it wasn't a gulp. He wouldn't admit to gulping. "I was waiting to be free." He stared at Sara Beth, willing her to understand.

She shook her head at him, then settled back down on the bed. "Idiot," she said.

He grinned.

∞

They chose the time for their confrontation with John carefully. The consortium had been a tremendous success. The news of Keane Industries'—meaning Ian's team's—breakthrough in AR research had exploded across the industry like fireworks on the Fourth of July. John was riding high on a triumph he hadn't earned, and it was time to pay the piper.

The man rubbed his hands together in anticipation as he walked into Alex's home office. "What did you need to talk about, Sara Elizabeth? This wouldn't happen to be the announcement I've been looking forward to for the last seven months, would it?"

Sara Beth's skin turned a little green, and Alex didn't blame her. The thought of allowing John access to a child after all they'd learned about him was sickening to him too. But John wasn't his father, and he couldn't imagine how hard this was for Sara Beth.

"No, Dad, I'm not pregnant."

John's scowl made his disappointment clear. "Then what?"

"Take a seat, John," Alex said. While Sara Beth sat on the couch opposite the one John deigned to occupy, Alex crossed to his desk and retrieved the folder he'd assembled from Corrine's information, as well as the follow-up he'd done through a team of private detectives. He took his time, girding his mental loins. When he finally took the seat next to Sara Beth, John was relaxed back into the couch, arms splayed as if he owned the place.

Looking at the man who had ruled such a large part of his life, Alex was surprised by the emptiness in his chest. He'd expected to feel something, anything, at this moment—anger, triumph, possibly even remnants of the fear that used to swamp him when he was a teen facing John's determination—but instead as he stared across the low table at the man who had run his life for so many years, only a weary resignation settled on his shoulders.

He got straight to the point.

"Sara Beth and I are getting a divorce."

The silence was thick enough to cut with a knife.

Then, "Like hell you will!"

"Yes, we will. You know Sara Beth is not happy, and neither am I."

John's derisive "So?" scraped along Alex's already tenuous nerves. Sara Beth's startled gasp telegraphed her hurt clearly.

"John—"

"Who gives a damn if she's happy, Alex? Really." John's disgust was evident as his gaze swept over his daughter. "I didn't marry her off to you to make her happy; I did it to secure the future of this company. This family."

"No, you did it to secure your power," Alex said. "Unfortunately for you, you picked a man who could care less about your power but cares everything about her happiness."

Into the uneasy silence that followed, Sara Beth spoke. "That's all I ever was to you, wasn't I? A means to an end." She choked on the last word, and pain speared Alex's chest. "You are my father. You're supposed to love me, not use me."

John didn't respond. They sat, the truth a suffocating presence between then, until finally John stood, giving them his back to pace across the room. When he turned, his gaze sought out Alex, not Sara Beth. Ignoring his daughter, he narrowed his eyes in speculation. "This is about that secretary, isn't it?"

Shit.

"You're going to throw it all away over a woman, a whore." John began a slow stalk back toward the couch. "Let me tell you something about women, Alex. They're faithless. The whole lot. Can't trust them as far as the next bed to hop into, and only then if you can tie 'em to it." He spread his hands along the back of the sofa and leaned in, emphasizing his point. "They're only good for one thing...or two things, actually." The gleam of humor in his eyes made Alex want to punch him.

"What's that?" he asked, knowing it was what the other man was waiting on, knowing the answer would make him sick.

"Securing the line, of course. And passing them on."

Alex fought the bile rising into his throat as John came around and made himself comfortable on the couch once more. "To someone like James Allen, you mean." He'd thought John would have a heart attack when Alex refused to try to convince Cailin not to testify. Only when he'd informed John the APD had plenty of evidence against the man even without her

183

as a witness had the backpedaling begun. Within days John had distanced himself and Keane Industries from Allen so far the Mississippi practically ran between them. But there was no distancing himself from the evidence in the folder Alex still held. There was simply too much of it, God help them.

"God, Dad…" Again that faintly nauseated tone in Sara Beth's voice. Alex reached for her hand, squeezing it, trying to infuse them both with strength. Sara Beth's rough swallow echoed in the still room. "I guess I should be thankful you didn't just sell me on the auction block."

Eyeing Alex, John humphed. "Might've gotten a better result."

Sara Beth stood abruptly. "I cannot believe my father is such a sick bastard!" Shaking her head, she asked, "Did you ever love me? Mom? Anyone but your own damn self?"

When John refused to respond, Alex told her, "At least you take after your mother."

The small hand holding his clenched, then relaxed as if in agreement. Alex had never wanted Sara Beth to hear her father say those things, but he knew now, it was for the best. Nothing less than the true sickness of John's mind could break the hold her father had on her belief in herself. The time for trying to please him had died long ago; they'd only waited this long for the burial.

Sara Beth seemed to sense the same, because she turned to Alex. "I'm done," she stated, eyes dry, clear. Resolved. "I'm done."

Alex nodded. Without a word to John, Sara Beth squeezed Alex's hand once more and walked out of the room. Silence hovered until the door clicked closed.

"She could've been trained into the perfect business wife, Alex. You're allowing her to walk out on the chance of a lifetime."

"For me or her?" Alex asked, disgusted. Without waiting for an answer, he shook his head. "I won't talk to you about Sara Beth any longer."

John continued to eye him, a general searching for the best place to attack. "You think she's something special, huh? Your blonde?" he finally asked. His tone said she wasn't.

"I won't discuss Cailin with you any more than I will Sara Beth." Just the thought of this man's opinions of the women in Alex's life made him want to gag.

"Alex, Alex, Alex...I taught you better than this," John crooned.

Alex nodded. "Yes, you did." *Or attempted to.* "And I'm happy to say I've forgotten everything you tried to drill into me."

"Your little secretary has been trouble since she first came aboard. Maybe more trouble than she's worth."

As if you can do anything about it. Aloud Alex asked, "You think your threats will work on me like they do helpless women?"

John snarled. "She can still disappear."

"So can you."

"Not as easily, you'll find."

Lunging across the table, Alex had John's tie twisted in his fist faster than John could blink. "Wanna bet?" Even John's lack of oxygen couldn't have communicated the threat better than Alex's stare. "She is mine. Stay. Away."

A harsh gasp, the struggle to draw in nonexistent air, filled Alex's ears; finally the twitch at the corner of his eye signaled John's understanding. His nod was overkill. Releasing the tie, Alex carefully smoothed the silk before sitting back.

"Looks like the people I surrounded myself with weren't as trustworthy as I thought," John said.

"We prefer being honest, not sleazy." He leaned forward in his seat. "The divorce is happening, John. There's nothing you can do about it; you might as well get used to it."

John was shaking as he finally let his own anger loose. "So be it. You can be replaced, you son of a bitch! I didn't train you all these goddamn years to—"

"Let's get something straight: you did not train me. You hounded me. What I learned, I learned from the best; I made sure of it. The only thing you taught me to do was hide."

"Hide? Hide what?" Venom hissed in the words.

"Myself." Alex threw the folder onto the table between them, and glossy, blown-up pictures and copies of documents spilled out across the gleaming surface. "But then, you know all about the subject, don't you, John? So I guess technically you *were* the best man to teach me."

John looked down, visibly reaching for control, and Alex saw the moment when he realized what he was looking at. Alex was careful not to drop his gaze—he had no desire to see the faces of the women John—and through him, Keane Industries—had betrayed. If it took him fifty years, every one of those women would be found. They would be compensated, cared for, and protected from the men who had abused them. Alex couldn't make up for what had happened—no one could—but if he had a snowball's chance in hell of ever sleeping again, even with Cailin beside him, he had to prove to them that he would never let it happen again.

One woman at a time.

John was slowly thumbing through the evidence. "Where in God's name did you get all this?" he growled.

Alex couldn't hold back his smirk. "Not God, John. You should know by now: a woman scorned isn't the only kind of woman you should fear."

The look John threw him could've steamed water. "There's no way—" Then his taut cheekbones paled. "Corinne."

Alex nodded. "She was a start."

"That sanctimonious bitch! She—" John's fists clenched, and his voice lowered to a register somewhere below mean. "You really think you can get away with this? I'll make her life a living hell."

As if I'm not smart enough to guess that. "It's too late, John." Thank God. "She's already here, under my protection—and you can't do anything about it. Not if you want to keep your secrets…secret." Carefully Alex reached out, thumbing aside the majority of the papers. At the bottom, where John had not yet ventured, lay the most damning evidence of all.

"Trina Marlowe." Alex picked up the woman's picture, studying it carefully. She'd taken the photo herself, it seemed, the night John hit her. Her pale image was a little blurred, but the black eye came through distinctly. Lord only knew what else the man had done.

Laying the picture directly in front of John, he picked up another. "Clarissa Johnson." The photo was set on top of the first, followed by a transfer order. A demotion.

The next picture was a redhead, her face holding a sickening resemblance to Sara Beth. "Mary Pantell."

On and on, the women John had had personal contact with came to light, in pictures and orders, lawyers' summaries for dropped lawsuits, bills from private detectives—"muscle," Corinne had called them. And the most damning evidence, witnessed testimonies, both from each woman and the people around them: coworkers, friends, health-care professionals, even spouses. Every sheet of paper built the ball of rage inside Alex until he was certain he could no longer contain it, until the probability that John wouldn't be leaving this building in one piece forced him to stop.

"Should I go on?" he asked, his voice a deep, dangerous threat.

"No."

With that single word, the man sitting across from him deflated, becoming in an instant the broken, powerless puppet he would remain from now on.

"There's nothing you can do, John. Give it up."

John tugged at the heavy knot of his tie as he cleared his throat. "What exactly do you want?"

"*We* want it all." No way would he leave John with any means of hurting a single soul more: not Sara Beth, not Cailin, not another woman, any woman. Period. He rose and crossed to his desk to retrieve another file, this one with paperwork from his lawyers. "You are going to retire." When John opened his mouth, protest imminent, Alex cut him off. "You will sign over your majority shares to Sara Beth, no caveats, no questions asked. Your *friends* will be stepping down, one by one, from the board, and their replacements will be chosen by a council headed by myself and appointed by Sara Beth and me."

"You can't—"

Using the new folder to nudge the old one, he pointed to the rest of the information, pages that held the stories of women hurt by John's cronies, men John had protected with Keane Industries resources. "I can."

"You bastard."

Alex's smirk was back. "I learned from the best, John." *What goes around comes around.*

John ranted and raved, and Alex let him, but in the end, they both knew the conclusion to this story. By the time John left, Alex had what he wanted, signed and sealed, witnessed and delivered. The nightmare was over.

The future was looking much, much brighter.

Chapter Fourteen

Ian planted a firm butt cheek on the edge of Cailin's desk and leaned down, his perfect blond curls framing a model-perfect face and perfectly green eyes. The man was sinful. After working as his secretary for almost five months, she'd thought she would get used to his good looks. Instead she'd marveled even more, especially as his resemblance to the little devil who sat on a cartoon character's shoulders became clearer and clearer. His personality had something to do with that, though, she figured.

"What are you wearing tonight?" he asked, looking down his perfect nose at her as she sat in the chair behind her desk.

"Huh?" She scooted her chair a little farther away.

He laughed. "The Christmas party, remember? What are you wearing?"

"Oh. Don't know."

Being Ian's executive assistant often reduced her to phrases. Pure self-preservation. Half the time she couldn't get a full sentence out without being interrupted.

"What do you mean, you don't know? I'm not missing the chance to see that ass in something besides baggy dress pants."

Without a word, she pointed to the half-filled jar on the corner of her desk. The label clearly read SEXUAL HARRASSMENT FUND in big, bold letters. Ironic considering sexual harassment was what had landed her in his office. When Corinne had moved, Alex and Cailin had decided she would step in as Alex's secretary and Cailin would move to R&D. It helped give them both the space they'd needed to stay distant at work while Alex and Sara Beth got both the company and their marriage settled. The transition had been accomplished smoothly, and overall the employees and investors—those who'd been allowed to stay, that is—seemed pleased with the changes. With a few bumps and bruises, Alex's plan had worked out great.

As had the jar. Every time a suggestive remark left Ian's mouth, she made the big flirt put a dollar in the clear plastic container. So far she hadn't bought the first lunch since they started the routine.

Fishing out his wallet with a loud sigh, he pulled it open. "All I've got is a ten."

"I'll take it."

"Of course you will." Muttering the whole time, he folded the ten-dollar bill and slid it through the slot cut in the jar's lid. "Now, the party?"

She shook her head. "Don't know."

Ian rolled his eyes to the ceiling and began to curse in what she assumed was Norwegian. His parents, he'd told her, were first-generation immigrants. They'd made sure their brilliant boy could speak both their native language and the language of their new home. Ian tended to only use the curse words.

While his eyes were otherwise occupied, Cailin allowed a smile to sneak onto her lips. One thing was certain: Ian made the days interesting, and he kept her from dwelling on the heartache she'd seen over the past few months. Alex's goal had been to track down every woman in Corinne's file, and he'd done that.

Helping Sara Beth work with them on everything from simple apologies or compensation to getting their lives back on track had filled both their nights and weekends, but it was worth every minute. If hearing the women's stories sometimes kept her up at night, at least now she had Alex to hold her close and keep her warm. Sane. Happy.

Among other things. Which was why tonight was making her so nervous.

"I'm pretty sure you've surpassed that ten you paid me a minute ago. Might want to switch to English and hush," she finally told him, trying desperately to hold back her laugh. She never laughed until he left the room. It only encouraged him, and he didn't need the encouragement; he needed a muzzle.

Ian laughed instead. That laugh always brought out a smile. She couldn't help it. The man just enjoyed life. When he reached for her hand, she set it easily in his. "You, my dear," he said, tugging her up from her chair, "absolutely have to look phenomenal tonight, no ifs, ands, or buts."

She jigged to the side. "Keep your hand away from my butt."

Ian leaned over her shoulder to eye said body part with a leering grin, but when his gaze returned to hers, he got serious quick. "Why the nerves?"

The man read women much too easily, that was for sure. With an exaggerated sigh, she gave in. "Alex is meeting me there tonight."

"And...?"

"And..." she mocked, "we're 'going' to the party together. As a couple." Openly. For the first time. Not that she needed to spell any of that out for him. Ian was one of only a few who knew the whole story by now, mostly because he'd figured out even before they had that she couldn't keep her eyes off Alex, and vice versa. She often thought it was one of the reasons he was so free with her, since there was very little doubt that she was taken with a capital *T*.

"Ah," he said. "No wonder you're nervous."

"Mmm," she murmured noncommittally. The sway of their still-joined hands reminded her of a game she used to play with her pigtailed girlfriends in elementary school. "People will talk."

He bent closer until their faces were on level with each other. "People always talk, Cailin. That's the way people are."

"Yes, it is."

"Right!" He dropped her hand and slapped his palms against his thighs. "So why not make them talk about something good for a change, like how fine your ass looks in that red dress you wore—"

Her hand clamped over his mouth with record speed. "Stop," she said, giggling. "You have gone way past that ten, buddy."

Sharp teeth nipped her palm, and when she let go, he said, "Did you doubt I would?"

"No."

"Of course not. I'm fabulous that way," he said with a girlie accent. "Now, mosey on home and put on the dress. It's perfect."

"How do you know? You can't possibly remember…" Her laughter faded as memories of the dinner party at Alex and Sara Beth's flooded her mind.

"Every man there that night remembers that dress, my dear. I am a man, you know."

No one would doubt that. "Ian…" Her stomach turned over. "I can't wear that dress."

"Why not? It's perfect. And red. And perfect."

Yes, it had been. Regret that Alex had never taken it off her mingled with anxiety at what had happened after that party. She shook her head. "I-I just can't."

Ian eyed her like a particularly difficult equation he couldn't quite figure out—a look she saw on his face often. She could almost see the lightbulb switch on when he connected the dots. His mouth softened, and he pulled her into his arms. His touch was tender, platonic. Ian was a touchy-feely kind of guy, so he'd gotten her used to his hugs early on. "Cailin," he said, the sound of her name almost a sigh. "We've worked together how long?"

"Too long." Her words were muffled against his shirt.

His chuckle vibrated in her ear. "Probably. You know me too well," he said with a light jostle. "The point is—"

"You have a point? You never have a point."

"Stop." More mumbled curse words, then, "The point is, I know things were rough between you and Alex and the Bastard—"

At the nickname he'd given John, Cailin leaned forward, put her mouth against the bulge of his biceps, and bit lightly. Ian yelped. They had a deal— no talking about John, even with euphemisms. He could talk to Alex about it all he wanted, but Cailin had dealt with too much of the aftermath; she didn't want to talk about the man any more than she had to.

Ian's next words came out cautiously, and she hid her smile as she listened.

"Anyway, I know it was a bad time. But let me tell you, seeing you that night in that red dress, seeing Alex seeing you, was something special. Something that can't, and shouldn't, be taken away by the Bas—" His hand came up to block her teeth from taking another bite. "Ow! Stop that!"

Snickering, Cailin stepped back. It really was a beautiful dress, and she really ought to wear it while she still could. The memory of the heat in Alex's gaze that night, the abandon with which he'd taken her afterward, sent a shiver down her spine.

One perfect, dark blond brow tilted upward as Ian waited for her response.

"Oh, all right. If I have to," she huffed, trying to sound as put out as possible. "Alex probably doesn't even remember it, anyway." As if that wasn't a fifteen on the lying Richter scale.

Alex evidently thought so too, because he snorted his opinion of her statement, then gave her a playful grin. "Wanna bet?"

∞

His searching gaze landed on the doorway just as she walked through, and the words he'd been about to speak evaporated. Everything around him—the lights, noise, people, everything—faded into the background and disappeared. There was only Cailin and the vision she made in that sexy red dress. Well, that, and the sudden pain in his groin as his cock stood to attention in the amount of time it took to run his gaze down her body and back up. God almighty, he was one lucky man.

His mouth watered as he took in her full curves, the beaded nipples clear through the thin material of her dress, her skin creamy gold even as she approached the bat-cave lighting of Thrice's bar area. After the freedom of having her the last five months, he'd have thought this unquenchable hunger would have leveled off, but no such luck. Adjusting himself discreetly didn't help the pain causing sweat to bead on his upper lip, and it certainly didn't help with his arousal.

The sound of a throat clearing, followed by a downright insulting laugh when he refused to look at Damien, finally drew his attention away from Cailin. "What?" he asked impatiently.

"I didn't say anything." Damien laughed outright, shaking his head. "Not that I wasn't thinking it. Damn, you've got it bad, my friend."

"Absolutely," Alex agreed with what he knew had to be a stupid grin.

"Just be sure not to pass it along," Damien whispered, leaning toward Alex so Cailin couldn't hear his words.

Just you wait, dickhead, he thought as Cailin took the last few steps into his outstretched arm. Gathering her close, he inhaled her sweet scent down deep into his lungs, and his erection jerked at the punch of vanilla and the curve of her hip brushing against his hard length.

"Hey, sweetheart."

An uneasy smile hovered on Cailin's lips, and her gaze darted to the groups of people nearby.

Nuzzling her ear, he whispered, "Relax. I'm here."

Cailin nodded but still didn't speak. Only one way to get rid of her nerves.

Alex lowered his head and took her mouth. The kiss he gave her wasn't discreet at all, but after her first startled "mmh," she didn't shy away. Her tongue played with his, and when he finally let go, hunger had replaced the anxious look from a moment before.

"Hey," she murmured breathlessly.

Mission accomplished.

Damien rolled his eyes, muttered something about Alex not being the only man in the room, and stepped in to kiss Cailin's cheek. "Hello, hon."

"Dam-i-en!" The last syllable rose in a disconcerted squeak as Damien gathered her into a hug—and settled his splayed hand a little too close to the rounded curve of her ass, or rather, *on* the rounded curve of her ass.

Growling at his friend, Alex extricated Cailin from his friend's hold and pulled her to safety. "Stop groping my girlfriend."

Damien flashed him a sly grin. "Can I move on to ogling then? 'Cause that is some dress." He pulled one of Cailin's hands out to the side and took in the full view once more. A low whistle puckered his lips. "Da-amn!"

Cailin shook her head at Damien's antics, a delighted sparkle in her eye. They talked for a few minutes about the Goth-style Christmas decorations the decorator had chosen to complement the club's sleek decor as they made their way over to the bar. Alex was seating Cailin on an end bar stool when one of the employees drew Damien aside. A word or two filtered back to them over the music.

"Sir…woman…you."

"Who?"

Alex couldn't catch the name, but the flash of anger darkening his friend's cool eyes said whoever it was hadn't been invited.

"What is it?" Cailin asked. Alex shook his head.

"…here…town…"

Damien hissed what Alex guessed from the look on his face were some fairly unsuitable words, then, "…busy. Get a number…"

"…insists…only you." The young man shrugged.

This time the "damn it!" was clear—and clearly pissed off. Damien turned to Alex and Cailin. "This can't be put off, sorry." He bussed Cailin's cheek, then nodded at Alex. "I'll see you later on tonight. You guys enjoy yourselves."

As Damien turned and headed toward the front, Alex looked beyond his friend's wide shoulders and caught a glimpse of a tall woman in a rocker outfit that would rival the most flamboyant Saturday night crowds at Thrice, a full sleeve of ink snaking up the arm closest to him. The woman met his gaze, then turned away, squaring her shoulders as Damien planted himself in front of her.

"Trouble in Thrice?" Cailin asked.

Alex shook his head, but he wasn't too sure. Shaking off the moment, he ordered his beer and a Coke for her. They took their drinks to a nearby table, and the swarm descended.

"Alex!" The hearty boom of Cade Ragen's voice fairly shook the tables. Part of the thriving Atlanta financial market, Cade was also one of the new board members at Keane Industries, filling the spot vacated by James Allen—may the bastard rot in jail.

Alex stood to shake Cade's work-roughened hands. Any man willing to get his hands dirty the honest way, Alex considered a vast improvement from the members of the board who'd "agreed" to his forced retirement plan. Ragen certainly fit the bill. "Cade, happy holidays."

"Now, down here we say merry Christmas and to hell with all that PC stuff." Tapping the brim of his Stetson, Cade greeted Cailin. "Hello, miss."

"My girlfriend, Cailin Gray," Alex said and gave Cade a warning glance when the man's eyes widened.

"Well now, it's a pleasure, Ms. Gray." Cade's gaze dropped briefly to the wedding band on Alex's right hand, the symbol of his marriage to Sara Beth. Alex knew the rumors: that he wore the ring because he couldn't let Sara Beth go, that they'd divorced because she'd refused to give him an heir. And those were the tame explanations. The gossipmongers had been busy—and way off the mark. Fortunately, curious or not, Cade kept his questions to himself and instead asked Cailin about her work.

The ring was the biggest question in everyone's minds. Why did he wear it still, yet not on his left hand, as he had before? Why did Sara Beth wear hers, even after her commitment ceremony two weeks ago with Sam? For Alex, it was simple. Their friendship had endured time and turmoil and come out the other end stronger than ever. Sara Beth was the reason they'd moved to Atlanta, the reason he'd found Cailin. He wore his old ring proudly. Watching Cailin describe Ian's latest crazy antics, Alex knew he also wanted her to wear his ring, and soon.

Cade exchanged more pleasantries, a bit of shoptalk about the planned production phase for their AR research, then moved on. His spot was quickly filled with a succession of employees, investors, friends, until Alex thought if one more person wanted to talk to him, he just might scream. When a brief lull finally arrived, he decided to take advantage of it.

Leaning into Cailin's space, he asked, "Wanna dance with me?"

"With you?" Cailin raised an eyebrow, which he promptly kissed. She swatted him away and stood. "Oh, okay, if I have to."

"Sweetheart, you're asking for it, you know that, don't you?" He started a slow stalk toward her.

Cailin threw a mischievous peek over her shoulder. "I thought you'd never notice."

CAILIN SASHAYED HER way toward the dance floor. Alex followed close behind, so downright gorgeous in his black tux with his dark hair trimmed and a new goatee gracing his firm chin. The skin along the sides of her neck tingled at the remembered feel of that soft, scruffy facial hair. She loved the easy scrape of it along her neck, her breasts, her thighs…

Her mouth went dry. She turned her head, chin tilted over her shoulder, and licked her lips.

Alex groaned.

Reaching a clear spot on the dance floor, she relaxed as Alex's arms circled her waist and his chest met her back.

"Cailin." Her name was a soft moan in her ear as she nestled her butt against his hips. "Sweetheart, this might be a really short dance if you keep that up."

"That's the idea."

He rubbed the soft bristles of his new goatee against her neck as he chuckled. "Brat."

He made her feel that way: daring and powerful, safe to do and say and be anything she wanted. Alex's boldness fed hers. Like now.

With Alex's palms flat against her abdomen, Cailin noticed a whisper of sensation as his thumbs brushed the undersides of her breasts—her fairly bare breasts. All that separated their skin was a thin film of silk. As she swayed, her breasts moved, her nipples rasping against the material, adding to the need building in her core. Alex's hips nudged hers, making it clear he was equally hungry. The knowledge that his touch was hers anytime she needed it settled the long-held doubts in her soul, healed the scars given to her in another life, one that was fortunately only a faraway memory now. Here, with Alex, there was only love, desire. Heat.

As that heat curled higher and higher, she began to wonder exactly how long she was expected to last. When one of Alex's hands slid down to press below her belly button, her core spasmed and she shivered, squirmed. No, it wouldn't be long.

Desperation had her turning around to press fully against his chest, trying to ease the ache in her breasts. She and Alex began a slow give-and-take, moving to the music, hands and bodies—and, occasionally, surreptitious lips and tongues— touching, sliding, gripping. Cailin could feel tension building in Alex's frame, his need obvious though he fought to keep them circumspect on the dance floor occupied by so many of his employees and their families. When her fingers inched to the buttons on his shirt of their own accord, he laid his hand over hers, stopping her, his wicked grin generating tingles in her lips as he brushed it against them.

"Are you trying to tell me something, sweetheart?" he asked.

"Yes." Her answer was low, hoarse.

"Hmm." Alex stroked two lazy fingers down her spine, tantalizingly close to her tailbone, then up, around, exactly the way he often stroked her slit when they made love. Her knees wobbled, and Alex chuckled even as he held her up. "Maybe we should go somewhere more private. What do you think?"

"Parking?" Attempting to wait the half hour it took to get home could be dangerous; she might jump him on the interstate.

Alex gave a slow, sexy shake of his head. He grasped her hand in his, intertwined their fingers, and led her nonchalantly from the dance floor.

As they climbed the stairs, Cailin saw Sara Beth and Sam standing near the bar. The soft glow of love lit their faces openly now, squeezing her heart. When Sara Beth caught her eye, she lifted her hand in a wave, winked at Alex, and went back to her conversation with Ian and Damien.

Alex led her around the railing and then stepped toward that long, dark hallway she remembered so well. "Where are we going?"

"You'll see."

Twenty yards. Ten. Before she knew it, they stood in front of Damien's office door. The dark metal surface brought back memories of nerves and need and, much later, pain. Cailin blocked them out. Tonight was for them. Now. Not the past.

Alex looked back over his shoulder, gave her a once-over that melted her bones, then took a key card out of his pocket.

She sucked in a breath. "You had that in there the whole time!"

"Of course I did." He swiped the card and led her inside.

Her impressions of Damien's office had been hazy—she'd spent all her time focused on Alex and the pleasure he'd given her; nothing else had mattered. Tonight she stepped into another world. On one side, the dimly lit room held a black lacquer desk and shelves that must be Damien's. The other side was a seating area, but the couch and chairs had been moved back to line the wall. In the middle of the space was a massive bed on a low frame. Candles lit every surface, flickering shadows across the creamy sheets.

Pillows mounded at one end, making her blush. Alex was good with pillows. She knew that. Just the sight of them had her going wet between her thighs.

When she lifted her gaze to Alex's, he was watching her intently.

"Why?" she asked, trying to hide the tremble of emotion in her voice with a heavy breath.

"Because I love you." He drew her toward the bed. "And because in those hot, sweaty moments with you here, in this room, our first time, you became mine." He seated her on the silky sheets and knelt before her. One hand went to his jacket pocket. "And because I can't think of a better place to start our new life together." He pulled out a small jeweler's box.

Tears stung her eyes as she fixed her gaze, not on the box, but on Alex. "Oh God." That wasn't Alex's playful stare, nor his sexy stare. That was the intent look he adopted when he was determined to get his way, come hell or high water. Every line of his face displayed the full expanse of his forceful will, all zeroed in on making certain he got exactly what he wanted.

And what he wanted was her.

The snap of the lid was crisp in the silence between them.

"Look," he ordered.

She dropped her eyes, her throat closing as she saw what awaited her. A slender silver band of tiny diamonds sparkled in the candlelight. At the front, an antique setting held four square-cut larger stones in a diamond configuration that gleamed like silver fire. It took her a moment to realize the diamonds sparkled more because the box was moving ever so slightly. Alex's hand, holding the ring for her perusal, was shaking.

"Oh, Alex." She reached out to cup his hand, steadying him. "I love you."

"Then marry me."

The depth of need in his eyes consumed her. There was only one answer she could give: "Yes."

He smiled that wickedly sexy smile, and she swore relief washed across his face. She'd tease him about it later, maybe. But right now all she could think about was the man in front of her. He took the ring from the box and held it up in the light for her to read the inscription.

"L" for loved. "A" for always.

He'd remembered. Late one night, they'd lain before the fireplace in his new house—their new house—and she'd talked about her "scarlet letters," all those sins that had made her who she was, that she'd realized weren't sins after all. Alex had kissed her chest right above her heart and told her letters would never do her justice; only his love could do that. And it had. Being loved unconditionally had freed her from the guilt of the past, freed them both. No more dirty little secrets, no more hidden shame. They were together, and they were loved.

"Thank you."

A single tear traced her cheek as Alex slid the ring on her finger. "For what?" she asked.

"For saying yes." He leaned in to kiss her.

She laughed softly. "Well, I kind of had to," she whispered against his lips.

"Why?"

"Because I have one more secret."

Alex drew back. "What's that?"

She shrugged, but her smile was so wide she thought her cheeks would split. "I'm pregnant."

Alex's stunned expression had her biting her lip. Moments passed, and he still didn't speak.

"I guess the specialist was right—the problem wasn't mine; it must have been Sean's."

"But...but we just... We've only tried a month!"

Nodding was the only response she could come up with, so she kept doing it, and laughing, and grabbing for Alex as he started to laugh.

"We did it! I knew we could do it!"

"Alex, it wasn't a race."

"Of course it was," he told her as he laid her back on the sheets and started to draw the slender strap of her dress off her shoulder. Leaning down, he stroked the bare skin at the exposed side of her breast with his soft lips. His goatee tickled as he said, "I don't know why I'm surprised. It was bound to happen fast—I can't keep my hands off you." And he proved it by nuzzling her breast, then taking the extrasensitive tip in his mouth and sucking deep.

"Alex!" Cailin bowed her back, feeding him more, digging her hands into his hair to hold him to her. Closing her eyes, she gave herself over to this man who knew her, heart and soul—her every desire, her every need. And now, every little secret.

∞

Did you enjoy UNAVAILABLE? If so, consider leaving a review at your favorite e-book retailer. And thank you!

Before you go...

Damien seems untouchable. Too bad he's about to meet his match!

UNDISCLOSED
Secrets 2

Business should never involve love—or secrets.

Harley Fisher irritated Damien on sight. Not because she was the cockiest know-it-all he'd ever met. No, it was because she was a *hot* know-it-all who did things to his libido that no employee should. Unfortunately his business needed her almost as much as he did.

He can't fault the quality of her work. And he can't resist her sassy mouth and perfect curves either. She's already deep in his heart when he discovers the secret she's been keeping all along, the secret that will destroy the life he thought he had.

And maybe, just maybe, put him back together again.

∞

"I honestly thought nothing could get better than book one in this series. Ella Sheridan is making a career out of proving me wrong. Gut-wrenching and powerful, *Undisclosed* is a love story with a twist…"

– Nice Ladies Naughty Books

∞

Chapter One

"You're who?"

Harley came very close to laughing, though she wasn't sure if it was actual amusement or just plain nerves. George Michael's voice crooned "Last Christmas" in her head. *"Tell me, baby, do you recognize me?"* *It's definitely been a year. Guess the answer's no.*

She managed to hold back the laughter. Barely. Nerves wouldn't get the better of her any more than Damien Adams would. She refused to allow it. Squaring her shoulders, she ignored the fact that she felt like an idiot with her hand dangling out in front of her, waiting to shake, while she faced down the man who had taken the Atlanta bar scene by storm less than a year ago. In person he was more like a blizzard, slamming into her senses, whiting out everything, including her courage. She'd always been good at faking it, though.

Ignoring his obvious impatience, she tried again. "Harley Fisher."

The jerk stared back silently, full lips pressed tight together, a dark brow cocked up in question.

Okay, she knew she'd interrupted him, but seriously… She raised her own brow, getting a little impatient herself and trying hard to control it. "We spoke on the phone. About the general manager's position," she reminded him carefully.

Damien looked at her still-extended hand; then, with casual deliberation, he crossed his arms over his wide, muscular chest. The silk of his shirt stretched to a fit that resembled plastic wrap. Pulling her gaze from the deep V of the open neck, she dropped her hand and refused to be intimidated. She needed this job, and she intended to have it.

A spark of recognition lit those river-brown eyes, and Harley swallowed hard against the heavy, dry lump in her throat until he said, "Right. You're the one I thought was a guy."

She caught her grimace before it could get out. Yes, her name was unusual. She was often mistaken for a man until someone saw her in person, after which they simply thought she was an airhead. Or a slut. Her youth and rocker-chick persona often worked against her in the "real" world, but it never took people—men—long to learn differently. Hopefully Mr. Slick here would be quick on the uptake.

From the look of it, she had a better chance of Santa coming down her nonexistent chimney.

Raising her voice slightly to be heard over the remixed Christmas song blaring from the speakers, she said, "Yes, that Harley." Try a smile, she told herself. "We—"

An impatient shake of his head cut off her words. "I believe I told you we were looking for someone more"—his gaze slid slowly down her body and back up—"more."

More what, for God's sake? More ready to jump into bed with him? A strong urge to put her leather jacket back on, as if she were still out in the Atlanta winter cold, bit into her. And pissed her off. Maybe she'd made a mistake in coming here. Damien obviously wasn't the man she'd thought he would be, the man she needed.

No, give it a chance. This is too important to be making rash decisions. He can afford to; you can't.

She dug her fingernails deep into her palms and wished her soon-to-be boss wasn't quite such an ass.

Or quite so sexy. Looking at him heated her body in a way that had nothing to do with the anger she was feeling. The reaction shook her. Of course, Sonny'd always had good taste in men.

Which was definitely not why Harley was here.

Pain tingling in her palms from the digging of her nails, she forced herself to hold his stare. "Mr. Adams, simply because I'm young—*and female*—doesn't mean I'm not the right person for the job. If you could just take a look over my résumé one more time—"

"I've seen what I needed to see, Ms. Fisher," he said, voice dropping to little more than a growl. "I own three very successful clubs in three cities hundreds of miles apart. Traveling between them means leaving someone else in charge, someone with the experience and expertise to work independently, wisely, and efficiently. It means I must trust that person implicitly with my livelihood and that of my employees. Being Thrice's general manager requires more than a familiarity with the bar." That insulting look returned to his eyes, implying various ways she might've gained such knowledge that had nothing to do with her brains.

Oh, he so did not go there.

"So what you're saying is, a woman in her midtwenties, a former musician, covered in tattoos but looking reasonably attractive is by definition a lush? Or are you insinuating that I'm a whore?"

Damien stared, eyes wide with shock, as if he couldn't believe the words that had left her mouth. Then a boyish grin transformed him from put-out businessman to dangerously naughty hunk, and the urge to let go of her anger sank its teeth deep. No way. She was not forgetting he was rude, egotistical, asinine, a dickhead...

He laughed before she could let a real hissy fit loose. The sound echoed, rich and full, blending and countering the music filling the room. It deflated the ball of emotion choking her, drew her in, made her want to mix her laugh with his. She held her breath, unable to decide if his reaction was a good or bad thing.

"Forgive me," Damien said. A wheeze interrupted the last word, and he had to pause to get his mirth under control. "You're right. That was uncalled for." Like an old-world aristocrat, he bowed from the waist. His shirt draped away from his chest, giving her a glimpse of smooth, tan skin all the way to his navel. "My apologies."

Did he plan to kiss her hand next? The man had throwing people off down to an art. And why didn't he look ridiculous with his shirt unbuttoned down to a lick-worthy six-pack? Reminding herself of her purpose, she said warily, "Accepted. I think."

His grin said if that was the best he could get, he'd take it. "Ms. Fisher, I appreciate your candor— and that you are willing to forgive my rudeness. But—"

She barely refrained from rolling her eyes. *There always has to be a but.*

"—the fact remains that a certain level of experience is necessary for this position. I'm sorry."

He turned to leave, and panic took over, pushing her to close the distance between them. Instinctively her hand shot out, and then she was gripping the heavy muscle of his biceps. Desperation firmed her hold when the shock of physical contact shot up her arm like a lightning bolt. He felt hot. Masculine. This close, he smelled of spice and alcohol, and she found herself breathing heavier just to take in more.

Don't be a damn fool, Harley! Get your act together.

"Ms. Fisher—"

Before he could blast her for detaining him, Harley firmed both her courage and her voice. "Thrice has been open how long, Mr. Adams?" When he refused to answer, she did it for him. "Six months. I've been involved in the Atlanta music scene for fifteen years, the last seven of which I spent not only as a musician but as an event organizer and PR rep for my band and several others."

That got him to face her fully. "You are either older than you look, or that's a big stretch of the truth."

She let a smirk sneak onto her lips. "And you are more unfamiliar with your new market than I would have given you credit for. My mother rotated out of every club in town, dragging me along with her from the time I was ten so she could sing her heart out. At fifteen I became involved with the indie music scene, and three years later formed and managed my own band, Aftershock."

At the name, Damien's brows shot up. *So much for actually reading my résumé.* Anyone with even a basic knowledge of indie music had heard of Aftershock; they were one of the foremost bands in the business, not just because they were damn good musicians, but because Harley had as good of instincts in management as she did with a bass guitar. If her private life hadn't blown all to hell, she would still be with them.

"I see."

She could tell he didn't like admitting he was wrong, but at least the playboy charm was darkening into something more serious, more thoughtful, without the annoyed edge he'd shown at first. Time to close the deal. "You know the national scene, no doubt about it. You know what needs to be done to make things happen in LA or Colorado. You gained that know-how through study, experience, and *local* help." She fought to keep the quaver of desperation out of her words. "I can give you that here, Mr. Adams, and with far more depth and speed and with lower cost than anyone else you could hire. I know Atlanta. I know the people here. I know the nightlife and the music and the contacts to make it all happen." She pulled in a heavy lungful of air to ease her aching chest. "*I* am the person for this job."

When the last word left her lips, she knew every ounce of her passion and determination went with it. Her lungs deflated like a balloon with a slow leak, refusing to refill as she waited for his verdict. Thinking of everything that was at stake, she willed him to listen, to see all that she could offer.

"You're not gonna give an inch, are you?" he finally asked.

Harley narrowed her eyes. "No, and you wouldn't want me to. It's exactly what you need."

Damien's gaze dropped to the hand still clutching his arm. Harley slowly released him, the burn of embarrassment firing her cheeks. When his mouth, that sinfully full mouth, opened to speak, she braced herself for rejection.

"Okay."

Wh-what? The single word hit like a brick wall she'd never seen coming. "Okay?" she parroted.

"Okay, let's talk." Glancing down, he surveyed the thick black watch encircling his wrist. "I have a couple of things to settle first, but if you're willing to hang around, I'll take the time to speak with you."

Clenching the muscles in her thighs to keep herself from slumping to the floor in relief, she forced calm into her voice. "Yes. Absolutely."

Damien stared down at her for a long moment, something dark and unreadable in his eyes. Knowing she had to get used to him watching her, judging her, she let him look. Whether he found what he was looking for or not, she didn't know. He turned to a passing employee, asked the man to escort her to a table in the bar, and nodded before making his way down a nearby hall.

She couldn't resist a final glance in his direction as she was led across the room. Step one down. They were on their way.

∞

He needed to stop looking at her. Every few minutes his gaze strayed toward the corner table in the bar where Harley Fisher sat, sipping a drink with red and silver sprinkles rimming the glass, chatting with every employee who passed. The Christmas lights illuminating the area glinted in her eyes, and he couldn't keep his fucking gaze off her. Which was bad, because he didn't do employees—ever. And he wanted to do her, no doubt about it.

Pretending to listen to Brad give him a rundown of the night's tally, he took in the picture she made. She fit, which was what had made him wary at first. Too young, too hip. From the top of her candy-red-

and-cream-striped hair to the toes of her knee-high stiletto boots, she looked like one of his customers— the ones he occasionally slept with—not a manager. She had slipped her tight leather jacket onto the chair back, revealing a silky silver tank that showcased a full-sleeve tattoo along one slender, toned arm. Those muscles came from holding a guitar, he now knew. A musician. Wasn't that just further reason to be panting after the woman? It was a wonder he hadn't been forced to roll his tongue back into his mouth like the cartoon characters he remembered from childhood.

"Boss?"

Brad's voice pulled him back to business, and Damien turned, removing Harley from his line of sight. Tonight's private Christmas party for Keane Industry's Atlanta office had been well attended, the bar busy all night. Brad needed his attention, as did a million additional things, both here and at his other two clubs. He needed a general manager for Thrice. Once, his club in LA, and Twice, the Denver nightclub, were both hugely successful, but he wasn't the kind of owner who could open a place and then leave it in someone else's hands entirely. He stayed in constant contact with both managers, flying out frequently to each location, this month in particular. The series of charity events planned for the holidays would benefit hundreds of families in the three cities where he ran clubs, but they added more strain to his already overfull schedule.

He and Brad were finishing up the details for tomorrow's order when Ryan strolled over to lean against the bar.

"Sounds good, Brad," Damien told the bartender. "Finalize those numbers and have Malik get that order in ASAP tomorrow morning."

Brad immediately pulled out his phone to shoot the day supervisor a reminder, which was one reason the man had become such a trusted employee so quick. He got things done and done fast. Damien needed all the help he could get. Fifty e-mails waited on his phone for his attention, and that didn't include the things Ryan, as his assistant, handled on his own, or the things Ryan couldn't handle when he and Brad took over Thrice while Damien was away. Both men worked hard, but neither had the know-how or experience to run the club without constant input from Damien, not yet. The need for a seasoned day-to-day manager here at Thrice neared desperation level at this point. No one he'd interviewed had felt right for such an important position, though. No one had even come close, not until Harley.

"Remind him about contacting that wholesaler while you're at it," Ryan put in. "See what the guy has to offer us."

Brad nodded, fingers flying, then hit a final button and looked up. "Anything else?"

"No, you're good," Damien told him, meaning it.

"Does that mean I get an extra-special Christmas bonus this year?" the bartender asked with a grin.

"I don't know. Ryan?"

Brad groaned. "You did not put Wonder Boy in charge of our bonuses, did you?"

"I'll remember that," Ryan warned.

Brad laughed as he headed toward the other end of the bar, which spanned the length of the club area, to finish supervising the night's cleanup.

Ryan leaned a little closer, brows up almost to his hairline, and smiled slyly. "So, who's the girl?"

In the four years Ryan had worked for him, Damien had come to love his young assistant like a little brother, so he didn't resist the urge to smack the little pissant upside the back of his head.

"Hey, man, don't mess with the hair!" Ryan smoothed the ruffled strands at his nape, but his smile widened despite the whine in his voice.

"Keep your tongue on a leash," Damien warned, his words lacking heat. Without his consent, his gaze traveled toward Harley, watching as one of the waiters approached her table to offer a refill. Harley shook her head; then something the man said made her laugh. A twinge of pain shot through his jaw as Damien ground his teeth together. "That," he told Ryan, "is Harley Fisher."

Ryan shot to attention at his side. "*The* Harley Fisher? From Aftershock? Hot damn!" His tongue practically hung out as he stared across the room, and Damien started to wonder if he was going to have to wipe up drool. "I didn't recognize her offstage. Is this my Christmas gift? Say yes. Please?" The last word definitely approached a whine.

Ryan was much closer to the indie scene than Damien, obviously, but it wasn't as if Damien had no clue who the woman was. Aftershock was one of those bands that even adamant anti-indie listeners knew and enjoyed. He kept up with their music, if not all the band members' names. What he did know was the venues they played—good ones, events that took finesse to get, especially for a band without the solid backing of a major record company. If Harley acted as their manager, she knew what the hell she was doing. So why leave that behind to work for him?

Ryan's gushing made the pain in Damien's jaw worse. "Down, boy. She's applied for the general manager's position."

"No kidding?" A thoughtful look crossed Ryan's boyish face. "I'd heard she was on hiatus. Maybe it was more serious than the rumor mill let on."

Something to think about. She certainly seemed the best choice overall, given her background. And if he was honest, the main thing holding him back at this point was the attraction he felt for her. He liked her spunk. He liked that she didn't take his shit without calling him on it. Damn it, he liked her, wanted her, and therein lay the problem. She was trouble waiting to happen. With a capital *T*.

A soft, feminine hand on his arm interrupted his thoughts. "Damien? Is everything all right?"

Mia. Another problem squeezing herself onto his overflowing plate. When he said he didn't do employees, he meant it, but Mia refused to get the picture.

He straightened. "Fine, Mia," he said, shifting as subtly as possible away from the petite waitress. Petite but strong, barracuda strong. She, like Harley, was young, maybe twenty-three. She'd been waitressing at Thrice for three months, and if things didn't change soon, he would be forced to let her go. Being ambushed every time he came in the door of his own club was unacceptable—and unavoidable. She'd made it so.

"Would you like me to gather the staff for the meeting?" she asked, swaying her shoulders side to side in an incongruously little-girl move that emphasized her generous breasts in the low-cut shirt she wore. Damien knew better than to look down. They were nice breasts—he'd noticed; he was a breast man, after all—but a single glance and he'd end up with a permanent attachment to his hip that would take a crowbar to remove.

Keeping his eyes firmly locked with her exotic, almond-shaped ones, he said, "Valentine will let you know when we're ready." He glanced over to see his waitstaff supervisor at the far end of the room, pointing two waiters in the direction of a section that had not been taken care of yet. He nodded in Valentine's direction. "Don't you have cleanup to get through?"

Mia's full lips pouted prettily. "I just wanted to help, Damien. I'm sorry."

Instead of rolling his eyes, he nudged his chin toward the opposite end of the room. "Finish up, please."

"That is a mess waiting to happen," Ryan murmured, barely waiting until Mia stepped out of earshot.

"I agree." He jammed both fists against the bar, arms rigid, and rolled his shoulders to release the tension that had settled there. "One you can take care of while I'm away."

"Thanks," Ryan mocked. "I get to cover your ass while you gallivant all over the country, *and* handle the horny waitress."

Damien smirked at the disdain dripping from Ryan's last word. "It's a dirty job, but at least I don't have to do it." Especially not at Christmas. Damien hated letting anyone go, but the young woman had been warned strongly and repeatedly. Knowing what had to be done didn't mean it depressed him less.

Damien motioned for Brad and Valentine to gather their crews for the "family meeting," the staff meeting held nightly to go over issues from the shift or things that needed to be addressed for upcoming ones. By the time they finished, Harley had been waiting more than an hour for his attention, but she didn't act impatient. She'd watched him handle the staff, those green eyes alight with interest. Now those same eyes narrowed on him as he walked toward her table, leaving Brad and Ryan to lock up.

Damien felt the pull of that look, right down to his groin. And that hair. Jesus. Her hair reminded him of those Life Savers strawberries-and-cream lollipops he used to love as a kid, a swirled mix of sharp tang and sweet, creamy goodness. It made him wonder where else on Harley he could taste creamy goodness. When his dick filled at the thought, he groaned. He needed her as a manager, not a good lay. He could get sex anytime; someone to fill the empty slot in his business was far harder to come by.

Harley was it, but neither he nor his cock were jumping for joy over the decision.

"Mr. Adams." Harley smiled as he sat across from her.

He dived right in. "Why do you want to work for me?"

A V formed between Harley's brows. "What?"

"Why me? Why Thrice? I know Aftershock's success, and I know the position I'm offering. I just can't figure out why you would go from that"—he cupped one hand, then the other—"to this."

A rosy flush crept up Harley's neck. She hesitated for so long he thought she might refuse to answer, but finally she spoke. "I left Aftershock six months ago."

"Were you fired?"

"No!" The indignation in her eyes convinced him quickly. "Some things happened…" Harley nabbed the swizzle stick from her nearly empty drink and twirled it, pausing a long moment before raising her eyes to meet his. "My sister died. I decided…" She shrugged. "I decided I needed a change. To be in one place, not a new one every weekend. Life's too short." A frown tugged one side of her mouth down. "I loved the band. I did. But it wasn't what I needed anymore."

Damien stared for a long moment before nodding. "Okay, I can accept that." There was no doubting the sincerity in her eyes. Not that he wouldn't verify her story—he'd already directed Ryan to run a background check.

"Thank you," Harley said. She met him look for look, seeming to drill a hole right through him. "You will not regret it if you hire me, Mr. Adams. I guarantee it."

He bet she would. And his every instinct screamed that he would regret it if he didn't hire her. The whole attraction thing, he'd simply have to ignore. "Call me Damien. We're going to be working together, after all."

Eyes lighting up, Harley leaned forward. "We are?"

"Yes, we are." Damien took his phone from his pocket and pulled up his calendar. "If you'll agree to a trial period, we'll see how it goes. Can you start

Monday morning?" That left him tomorrow to get his libido under control, though it would probably be an ongoing process.

"Certainly."

He forced a grin back, forced himself to stay focused on business even though his new potential manager practically bounced in her seat. Enthusiasm was good, if he could ignore what the movement was doing to her breasts. Trying to bring them both back to earth, he started in on his spiel about businesslike behavior. More than one employee had assumed because they worked in a club, the standards of professionalism would be lax. He didn't fear such a thing happening with Harley, who must have worked with managers in venues and nightclubs across the country, but the reminder of her purpose there—which wasn't to get in his pants—was something he needed.

Nearing the end of his speech, his attention caught on Harley's hair as she ran her hand through the messy locks. The sight of the damn stuff practically had him salivating, a reaction that absolutely had to stop.

"You need to dye your hair."

The words were out of his mouth before he knew what he was saying. Every part of him rebelled at the idea, which, perversely, made it even more necessary.

Harley frowned. Apparently she liked the idea about as much as he did. "It is dyed."

"It's not professional." And he was all about professional, wasn't he? Even if the heat in his gut said otherwise.

"It is in this business." Harley leaned forward on her elbows, almost nose to nose with him across the small cocktail table. "Look, I'll do a lot of things for you, but unless you want my hair purple when I walk into your office Monday morning, you won't insist on this."

"You wouldn't." Oh yes, she would.

Propping her chin on one hand, she shot him a mischievous grin that confirmed his suspicions. "I wouldn't?"

Shit. It wasn't like he could say, *Your hair makes me want to lick you all over.* Maybe he needed to hunt down some of those suckers and keep them in his office—or get out of town as soon as possible. The latter seemed the best alternative.

"Fine," he said, more than aware of his surly-ass tone. "No purple." Knowing his luck, he'd get a sudden craving for grape Tootsie Pops.

Harley stood, satisfaction radiating off her. "No purple, I promise." She winked—actually winked—at him, and he had to fight back a groan. The next few weeks were going to be hell; he just knew it.

Holding out a hand, Harley waited. Remembering his refusal to shake with her earlier, Damien reached out, knowing it was a mistake, knowing he should avoid touching her at all costs, and grasped her slender hand in his. The power of the contact shocked him—and her, if the gasp that escaped was anything to go by. For a single moment, their eyes met, and he saw his own overpowering attraction reflected back at him. Then Harley blinked and the moment was gone.

"Good night, Damien. I'll see you Monday morning—without the purple hair."

∞

Pick up your copy of *UNDISCLOSED* at your favorite retailer today!

About the Author

Ella Sheridan never fails to take her readers to the dark edges of love and back again. Strong heroines are her signature, and her heroes span the gamut from hot rock stars to alpha bodyguards and everywhere in between. Ella never pulls her punches, and her unique combination of raw emotion, hot sex, and action leave her readers panting for the next release.

Born and raised in the Deep South, Ella writes romantic suspense, erotic romance, and hot BDSM contemporaries. Start anywhere—every book may be read as a standalone, or begin with book one in any series and watch the ties between the characters grow.

Connect with Ella at:
Ella's Website – ellasheridanauthor.com
Facebook – Ella Sheridan: Books and News
Twitter – @AuthorESheridan
Instagram – @AuthorESheridan
Pinterest – @AuthorESheridan
Bookbub – Ella Sheridan
E-mail – ella@ellasheridanauthor.com

For news on Ella's new releases, free book opportunities, and more, sign up for her monthly newsletter at ellasheridanauthor.com.

Made in the USA
Coppell, TX
13 January 2023

11048906R00132